FROM THE JUNGLES OF SOUTH AMERICA TO
THE SANDS OF ANCIENT EGYPT, THERE'S
NOTHING OLDER THAN EVIL. . . .

INDIANA JONES—In the lost Mayan city of Cozán, Indy heard the curse of the Crystal Skull: "You will kill what you love." Now, he is looking for a missing alchemist's manuscript—and the curse is dogging his every step.

LEONARDO SARDUCCI—This brilliant and cunning conspirator is working for Mussolini's secret police. But is there a dark connection between the Italian dictator's quest for absolute power and the expedition of Indiana Jones?

ALISTAIR DUNSTIN—The world's leading authority on alchemy, he is rumored to be one of the few practitioners of the ancient art who can actually turn lead into gold. Indy strongly suspects that Dunstin stole the Voynich Manuscript, but not before performing his greatest trick of all: vanishing into thin air.

ALECIA DUNSTIN—The shy librarian and "reluctant psychic" was Alistair's closest confidante. She believes her mysterious brother is the innocent victim of a kidnapping and she'll do anything to convince Indy . . . even if it means keeping a secret that could get them both killed.

ITALO BALBO—The charismatic Italian aviator is a hero in his homeland. But at his command is an elite and brutal cadre, including one deadly saboteur whose target is the dirigible *Macon*—and the adventurer Indiana Jones.

INDIANA JONES™

AND THE

PHILOSOPHER'S STONE

MAX McCOY

BANTAM BOOKS
NEW YORK · TORONTO · LONDON · SYDNEY · AUCKLAND

INDIANA JONES AND THE PHILOSOPHER'S STONE

A Bantam Book / May 1995

All rights reserved.
TM, ®, and copyright © 1995 by Lucasfilm Ltd. All rights reserved.
Used under authorization.
Cover art copyright © 1995 by Lucasfilm Ltd.
Cover art by Drew Struzan.
No part of this book may be reproduced or transmitted in any form
or by any means, electronic or mechanical, including photocopying,
recording, or by any information storage and retrieval system,
without permission in writing from the publisher.
For information address: Bantam Books.

If you purchased this book without a cover you should be aware
that this book is stolen property. It was reported as "unsold and
destroyed" to the publisher and neither the author nor the
publisher has received any payment for this "stripped book."

ISBN 0-553-56196-0

Published simultaneously in the United States and Canada

Bantam Books are published by Bantam Books, a division of Random House, Inc. Its trademark, consisting of the words "Bantam Books" and the portrayal of a rooster, is Registered in U.S. Patent and Trademark Office and in other countries. Marca Registrada. Bantam Books, 1540 Broadway, New York, New York 10036.

PRINTED IN THE UNITED STATES OF AMERICA

OPM   13   12   11   10   9   8   7   6   5   4

In memory:
Denholm Elliott
(1922–1994)

*There are more things in heaven
and earth, Horatio, than are dreamt
of in your philosophy.*
— *Hamlet,* Act I, Scene 5

*All haile to the noble Companie
Of true students in holy alchemie
Whose noble practice doth men teach
To vaile their secrets with mistie speach.*
— *The Vicar of Malden*

Prologue

CITY OF THE DEAD

March 21, 1933
British Honduras

The sun emerged as a disk the color of molten iron in the notch between two darkly brooding and unnamed peaks of the Maya Mountains, bathing the mist-shrouded valley below in a ghostly half-light. As Indiana Jones watched, the outlines of a city materialized from the haze. A cluster of squat, chalk-white buildings surrounded a spectacular four-sided stepped pyramid and its adjacent acropolis.

"The lost city of Cozán," Indy whispered, more to himself than to the Guatemalan guide beside him. "Last seen by Sir Richard Francis Burton in 1867, then swallowed again by the jungle. Burton got out, but his friend Tobias didn't."

"It is a bad place," Bernabé said.

"They all are," Indy said.

The rays of the sun were already skimming over the acropolis and striking the Temple of the Serpent, atop the pyramid, above the blanket of mist. Filtered through the stelæ—upright stone pillars bearing hieroglyphs of important dates and rulers—the light produced an undulating pattern at the top of the steps on the pyramid's side, resembling nothing so much as a snake beginning to make its way down the Great Staircase toward the Sacred Well. When the snake reached the bottom of the pyramid, according to legend, the hiding place of the goddess of death would be revealed.

"Come," Indy said, pushing through the last of the rain-forest undergrowth and emerging at the perimeter of the city. "We have until the serpent reaches the bottom—ten, maybe twelve minutes. *Hurry.*"

Bernabé reluctantly followed. He was wishing he had not taken the gringo's money to lead him to the forbidden city of his ancestors, wishing that he had remained in his village with his round-faced wife and three children. The thought of never seeing them again sent a quiver down his spine.

"Señor," he called. "You have not forgotten our agreement that I am to remain aboveground. . . ."

If Indy heard him, he did not show it.

For two weeks they had followed the *sacbob,* the ancient Mayan highways paved with white stones, through heavy jungle to reach this forgotten valley— after spending months in research and more than a little of the museum's money in a few well-placed bribes to archivists and Central American officials—with just minutes to spare. There was no time now to follow any plan, only to plunge ahead and hope for the best—or to wait thirty-three years for the vernal equinox of 1966.

As they hurried down the Street of the Dead, the city's main thoroughfare, Indy thought of the thousands of people who had lived and died within the somber stone buildings; they had raised families, worshiped in the shadow of the pyramid, and even seen their blood run from the stone altar atop the pyramid. Three times a century they had watched the serpent god make its way down the staircase of the pyramid, just as he was watching now. Then one day they vanished. An entire civilization simply disappeared, leaving . . . ghosts?

Indy stopped.

On the sides of the pyramid, atop the other buildings, and across the courtyard, things were *moving.* There was the sound of whispers and low murmurs, and an occasional shriek that pierced the morning air like the cry of a jaguar. The serpent was a third of the way down the steps of the pyramid and the city had come alive once more.

Bernabé, who had caught up, crossed himself.

"The souls of my ancestors," he said reverently.

Indy laughed. The explanation was simple.

"Not unless your ancestors are monkeys," he said, pushing forward once more. "They're howlers, that's all."

"Howler monkeys—even worse," Bernabé said. "Gods of writing, gatekeepers of the underworld. The souls of our priests come back as howler monkeys."

They broke through the undergrowth onto the broad flagstones of the courtyard. The monkeys scurried away with backward glances and bared fangs, screeching cries of warning as they went. In a moment all of the howlers were gone.

"Not very brave," Indy snorted.

Without warning, one of the monkeys dropped from a tree and sank its teeth into the side of Bernabé's neck. Bernabé screamed in horror and spun around, trying vainly to pull the silver-tipped monster off his back. The monkey threw its head back and uttered a mournful howl through bloodied fangs.

Too frightened to speak, Bernabé's eyes pleaded with Indy.

"Hold still," Indy commanded. In one motion he uncoiled his whip and lashed out. The tip rent the air near the monkey's head with a resounding *crack!* and the animal dropped away, startled but unhurt.

Bernabé clutched at his bleeding neck.

"It's just a scratch," Indy assured him.

Bernabé addressed the monkey as it disappeared into the canopy of the rain forest: "Grandfather, you should have bitten *him*. He is the one who insulted you."

Indy looked back at the pyramid.

The serpent was halfway down the steps.

Indy knelt on the flagstones and sighted along his outstretched arm, extending in his mind's eye the path of the serpent to the base of the pyramid—which of the five doorways was it angling toward? The doorways looked identical, but only one of them would lead to the Sacred Well. The others were to be avoided.

"The frustrating thing," Indy said, more to himself than Bernabé, "is that you can't wait for the shadow to reach the bottom, because then it's too late—the goddess has already been revealed." He scratched his stubbled chin. "And you can't count on using the same doorway that somebody did before, because the doorways change."

Yet it appeared that if he followed the serpent's nose straight down the steps, it was heading directly for the middle doorway. But, Indy discovered as he watched carefully for a moment, there was a definite drift to the north. It had to be one of the two doors on the right. At least that narrowed the odds to fifty-fifty.

Indy set down the sixty-pound pack that he had carried for the last three days. He untied the flap and took out a fifty-foot coil of rope, which he slung across his body, and a carbide lamp. He shook the lamp to make sure there was plenty of fuel and water in it, then struck the flint several times. It wouldn't light. Damn, he cursed under his breath, why hadn't he brought a battery-powered light? He took a breath, forced himself to relax, and tried again, this time striking the flint slowly and deliberately. The flame burned brightly in the middle of the reflector.

Indy smiled.

"I desire my bonus now," Bernabé said.

"Huh-uh," Indy said. "When I come out, then you get your bonus. Not before." The look on Bernabé's face showed Indy that he wasn't counting on it.

Indy placed a finger in the middle of Bernabé's chest.

"You wait right here. You keep your eyes and ears open—I think we've been followed since yesterday afternoon. And you'd better hope I come back out, because if I don't, I'm going to tell your ancestors in the underworld how you've been mistreating their monkeys."

Indy turned toward the pyramid.

"Wait, señor," Bernabé said, regarding the five portals grimly. "You must not go into the Sacred Well. It is very bad. There is a curse."

"There always is."

Indy looked at his watch, then back at the serpent. It was a little more than halfway down, perhaps sixty percent or so, meaning that there were five, perhaps six minutes remaining.

He adjusted his fedora, straightened his leather jacket, and chose the second portal to the right. In a moment he was in darkness. It was cold and damp in the passageway, and the air was heavy with the smell of niter. The floor slanted sharply downward, and he proceeded as quickly as he dared, with one arm sweeping cobwebs away from his face. The carbide lamp showed that the passage was smooth and well made—one would be hard-pressed, he thought, to insert a knife blade between the blocks—and there were no glyphs or decorations upon the walls, only an unusual bright green moss on the floor.

Indy was thirty feet inside when his right foot slipped out from under him and he landed on the seat of his pants. He got to his feet and took a few cautious steps farther, slipped again, then realized the moss on the floor of the passage had become as slick as ice. He turned, scrambling to climb back up, but it was no use— now he was sliding backward down the passage. He tried bracing himself with his hands, but the corridor was too wide to reach both walls. He thought of the whip, but that was only ten feet long, and while the rope was long enough, there was no way to heave it back outside. . . .

Outside, Bernabé was staring up in horror at the serpent of light and shadow. It had descended low enough that it now was clearly heading for the farthest right portal—not the one Indy had selected. What *was* slithering down Indy's doorway was the tail of the biggest anaconda Bernabé had ever seen.

Indy watched as the blocks in the wall slid past at an ever-increasing pace. He rolled to the left and attempted to grasp the wall with his fingers, but succeeded only in breaking a fingernail, which made him curse. He was picking up speed and he knew that wherever the passage led, it couldn't be good; looking past the toes of his boots confirmed it. The flickering light of the carbide lamp revealed that the passage was about to end in an abyss. And the walls were so smooth one would be hard-pressed to—

"Knife blade!" Indy shouted.

In a moment he had drawn his hunting knife and was dragging the point against the wall, leaving a trail of sparks behind. The point came to a crack, hesitated for a moment, then continued. There were only two blocks left. Indy twisted the blade to gain a better angle. The knife went solidly into the joint—then the tip of the knife broke off and Indy was sliding again.

"Three's the charm," he huffed.

With herculean effort, Indy drove the broken blade of the knife into the last joint. It held, bringing him to a stop with a jerk that left his feet dangling over the abyss.

Carefully, working with one hand and holding on to life with the other, Indy used the butt of his revolver to pound the knife deeply into the joint. Then he tied the end of his rope several times around the handle guard of the knife, and cautiously lowered himself down to have a

look into the pit. The lamp did not give off enough illumination to see the bottom. There was the sound of water below him. Indy spit, and counted the seconds until
the splash. The hole was more than a hundred feet deep.

The passage Indy was following had ended, but the
lamp did show a hole in the left wall of the pit, approximately twenty feet down. Indy made sure he had a good
grasp of the rope, then began to lower himself down.
Then, when he was level with the opening, he pushed
off with his legs and began swinging himself like a pen-
dulum. On his second try he grasped the lip of the opening and pulled himself into it. It was a short lateral
tunnel that connected to another passage that ran east
and west.

Apparently, Indy told himself, the five portals were
connected in some intricate—and macabre—fashion
that used hydraulics and the height of the local water
table to determine which passage was traversable.

He looked at his watch. Time was short.

This passage also slanted down, but not as sharply
as the first—and with none of the deadly moss. Indy
paid out a few yards of the rope, which was still attached
to the knife handle, then burned through it and coiled
the remaining twenty feet or so over his shoulder. He
was still standing next to the pit when he heard the
sound of something or someone falling, followed a few
seconds later by a terrific splash in the pit below.

"Bernabé?" he called.

The name echoed back from the pit.

Indy was puzzled—surely there would have been a
shout for help or at least a scream if Bernabé had fallen.
He shrugged. Perhaps it was one of those infernal monkeys.

He moved on.

The passage narrowed, continued downward, and narrowed again.

Soon Indy found himself walking hunched over, then crawling on his hands and knees. As the passage narrowed, it became damper as well, until finally he was moving through six inches of foul-smelling water. Then the water came up to his chin.

At least, Indy told himself, he knew how deep he was: he had reached the level of the water table in the pit, which would also be the level in the Sacred Well.

He was crawling awkwardly with only one hand, because his right hand held the lamp up out of the water. Finally the passage began to climb again, and Indy smiled. Then he looked down at his hands and discovered they were spotted with dark blotches. He tried to rub the spots away, but they were attached in a rather rude way to his skin.

The water had been infested with leeches.

He plucked as many of them as he could from his hands and face, and grimly resolved to deal with the rest later. There were only two minutes left. When the passage opened wide enough, Indy ran. Triggered by his footsteps, a trio of thousand-pound stones fell, one after another, from recesses in the ceiling. They struck the floor where Indy had just been with a thunderous sound that reverberated deep in his gut. As the last stone fell Indy lunged forward.

The passage ended and Indy spilled out at the edge of the Sacred Well—a cenote, a limestone sinkhole formed in the recesses of the geologic past. The water glowed a faint blue, apparently from reflected sunlight, although the roof of the grotto was dark, and by that dim illumination Indy could see that the edge of the water was littered with what appeared to be white piles of balls and sticks.

As Indy got closer he realized with dread that the balls and sticks were human skeletons. He knelt down beside a pair of them.

One was the yellowed skeleton of a woman, undoubtedly a princess or the consort of a king, judging from the jewelry that had adorned her. An obsidian necklace and jade wrist and ankle bracelets were mingled with the scattered bones. There were also dozens of tiny copper-and-gold alloy bells, with the strikers removed—making them "dead" and therefore ready to accompany a princess on her journey to the underworld. Indy picked up one of the fragile radial bones.

"You had slender wrists, Princess."

From the mineralization that had occurred, Indy guessed that the skeleton was at least eight hundred, perhaps a thousand years old. All of this was typical of Mayan sacrifices of the late-classic period, Indy noted, except for two things: the skull was intact, but the rib cage had been crushed. A traditional ceremony would have required the priests to bash her head in methodically before throwing her to the god of the cenote.

The other skeleton was much whiter.

It was that of a man, in clothes that had been fashionable during the Victorian era, now just rags. He had been surprised in the act of robbing the princess, Indy knew, because some of her jewelry was stuffed into the rotting pockets of his frock coat. Like the others, his rib cage had been crushed. An ancient cap-and-ball revolver lay next to the bones of the right hand. Indy picked up the gun and inspected the cylinder. All six chambers had been emptied.

"Tobias," Indy said. "What could have done all of this?"

There were scores of skeletons around the cenote, and undoubtedly more in the water, but none of them could speak. Most of the dead, however, were concentrated in the area where Indy stood, although there seemed to be no altar or anything else nearby.

The water had been getting decidedly brighter. Indy looked at his watch. It was time. The serpent would be reaching the base of the pyramid by now. He felt a sense of impending danger, and he dropped the rusted and useless gun and drew his own .38-caliber revolver from the flap holster at his side.

A shaft of light burst from the ceiling of the grotto and, starting at the far edge, moved across the surface of the water. The water was so clear, and the light so intense, that Indy could see bones and bits of jewelry shining on the sandy bottom.

The beam moved steadily toward Indy.

Still holding the revolver, he ducked, letting the light pass over him. It struck the wall behind him, illuminating a skull of pure crystal set on an altar in a niche that would otherwise have remained hidden in shadows. Shafts of spectrum-tinged light shot from the skull's eyes and mouth, burning so brightly that Indy shut his eyes against the brilliance.

Then the light was gone.

The only illumination was from Indy's carbide lamp.

Indy holstered his gun, stepped gingerly among the piles of bones toward the altar, and crouched in front of the skull. It was the size and shape of a genuine skull, rendered chillingly lifelike by some long-dead artist's attention to detail, including the zygomatic arches of the upper cheeks and an articulated lower jaw with a perfect set of teeth. And, Indy noted from the brow ridges, the skull was feminine.

Indy inspected the altar for traps and, satisfied there were none, lifted the skull with both hands.

Nothing happened.

"This is too easy," he said.

"Yes, Dr. Jones, it is."

Indy glanced carefully over his shoulder. A Mauser automatic pistol was being pointed at the small of his back by a tall bald man in the characteristic brown suit and tie of the Fascista. An angry red scar ran across the bony crown of the man's head. The uniform was smeared with mud. In the hand opposite the man's gun hand was a kerosene lantern. A leech clung to one side of his bald head. He smiled, revealing a front incisor made of gold.

Behind the bald man was a thug in a gray uniform with black piping, holding a rifle on a terrified Bernabé. There was another lantern at the thug's feet.

The bald man put his lantern on the ground and took the revolver from Indy's holster and the whip from his belt. He tossed the gun into the water. The whip he threw a few yards away.

Then he seized the Crystal Skull.

"Ah, behold the unnamed goddess of death—ancient beyond imagination. Such extraordinary craftsmanship. Note the anatomical detail, Dr. Jones. She is quite unlike anything the Maya ever produced. They had no sense of the mimetic." He gazed wistfully into the depths of the skull. "No, this is the work of a previous and unknown civilization, one with skills far superior to the Maya—and, I daresay, to our own."

"Whoever you are," Indy said, "you're obviously a sucker for fairy tales."

"Forgive me," the bald man said. "What could I have been thinking? In my excitement I forgot that we haven't been formally introduced. Leonardo Sarducci, at your service." Without lowering the gun, he came to attention and clicked his heels together. "It would be imprudent to reveal more."

"Can't say that I'm pleased to meet you," Indy said, still eyeing the barrel of the Mauser.

"Oh, but I am pleased to meet *you*," Sarducci said. "I have followed your checkered career with some interest. You are at Princeton University now, is that not correct?"

Indy nodded.

"Ivy League! How splendid," Sarducci said. "Finally you are getting the respect you so badly desire. What a shame that you won't be around long enough to enjoy it. And scoff about fairy tales if you will, Dr. Jones, but the skull—she holds the secret of eternity itself. It would have been a crime to let you keep her."

Sarducci slipped the skull into a cloth bag and pulled the drawstring with an air of finality.

"Black magic, eh? I thought that stuff went out with Paracelsus," Indy taunted. "Say, if you're so smart and I'm so dumb, why couldn't you get in here without following *me*?"

"It was—how do you say?—expedient." Sarducci threw his head back and laughed, and the sound echoed from the walls of the grotto. Then he reached up and plucked the leech from the side of his pate. It left an ugly red wound. He flicked the parasite from his finger to the ground, then ground it into the mud with the toe of his boot. "In the same manner," he said, "now your death is expedient. Marco, shoot them both, but wait until I am gone—the sound of gunfire in such a closed place is bad for the ears, no?"

Sarducci, holding the lantern, and with the sack containing the skull slung over one shoulder, paused at the lip of the passage.

"What do you believe in, Dr. Jones?" he asked. "Do you trust in an afterlife, that death is merely a doorway—or do you believe, as I do, that death is utterly final, that the only way to cheat death is to live forever?"

"Guess," Indy said.

Sarducci chuckled.

"No, as an American you *would* believe in a Sunday-school afterlife, would you not? Just think—you are about to face the supreme test of your faith! I will think of you in the centuries to come, while I am enjoying the best that life and power have to offer and you are but dust."

He threw Indy an exaggerated salute.

"*Arrivederci*, Dr. Jones!"

Sarducci disappeared.

"Over there," Marco ordered, gesturing with the barrel of the gun. Hands high, Bernabé walked over and stood dejectedly by Indy.

"Can't we talk this over?" Indy asked.

"Shut up!" Marco barked.

"There's really no reason to be angry," Indy said, palms outward, edging toward Marco.

"Stop!" Marco cried, and sent a round into the mud

at Indy's feet. The report loosened dust from the ceiling. "Both of you, kneel down. Hands behind your head. Now."

Bernabé fell to his knees. Indy began to back away with a look of utter horror.

"Holy St. Patrick . . ."

At the edge of the lantern light, behind the thug, Indy saw something big and green slithering out of the water.

". . . I thought you'd want to know . . ."

Marco brought the rifle to his shoulder and put the sights on a spot between Indy's eyes. Coward, he thought. His finger began to tighten on the trigger.

". . . that the biggest damn *snake* I have ever seen is right behind you."

The rifle barrel wavered as Marco looked around. A thirty-eight-foot anaconda was staring at him, mouth open, forked tongue flicking out, rows of teeth gleaming in the lantern light. The green milky eyes were filled with reptilian calm. The head was scarred with old gunshot and knife wounds.

Marco screamed. He tried to bring the rifle to bear on the snake, but the anaconda was too fast; in less than a second it crossed the distance between them, knocking the gun barrel aside as it struck. Three shots went impotently into the mud as the serpent sank its fangs into the flesh of his left thigh. Now that it had a hold on him, the anaconda began turning Marco over and over, wrapping its coils around his torso.

"I hate snakes," Indy said. Sweat dotted his forehead, his lips quivered, and his hands began to tremble.

Marco no longer had the breath to scream. Each time he breathed out, the snake tightened its grip, and

his lungs were no match for the steel grip of the anaconda. Marco's face was purple and contorted in a silent,
pleading grimace. The stock of the rifle, which he still
held, cracked as the snake began to squeeze tighter. A
trickle of blood ran from the corner of Marco's mouth.

Indy turned away.

"Boss," Bernabé pleaded. "Isn't there something
we can do?"

"He's already dead," Indy said.

The anaconda opened its hinged jaw wide and engulfed the head and shoulders of the lifeless Marco. It
glided the body down on a coating of saliva, and when
only the shoes remained, it disappeared into the cenote.

"It saved our lives," Bernabé said. "Now it is gone."

"For now," Indy said. He wiped a sleeve across his
face and tried to slow his breathing. "But it will come
back for us. If we don't kill it, amigo, it will finish us
before we're halfway up the passage."

"But how?" Bernabé asked. "We have no weapons. . . ."

Indy extinguished the flame of the carbide lamp
and shook it to make sure it had plenty of fuel. Then he
unscrewed the fuel reservoir at its base one half turn.

"I know people who fish with this stuff," Indy said,
trying to control his voice. "It explodes on contact with
water. I hope it works the same—"

Bernabé pointed.

The green-and-yellow head of the anaconda was
weaving its way toward the surface. Now free of its burden, it was moving quickly.

"Grab the lantern," Indy said. "Don't let it go out.
As soon as I throw this thing, run for the passage."

Bernabé picked up the lantern.

When the anaconda was within fifteen feet of the surface, Indy lobbed the carbide lamp into the water. It sank quickly, a flurry of gray bubbles coming from the loosened fuel reservoir. Indy ran toward the passage, snatching up his whip from where Sarducci had thrown it.

The explosion was deafening and lit the interior of the grotto in a ghastly pink light. Chunks of meat and pieces of green, black-spotted skin rose on a geyser of water, followed by a golden, slitted eye the size of a grapefruit. A dark stain blossomed in the depths of the cenote.

Indy, crouched in the passage entrance, said a silent prayer of thanks. Behind him, Bernabé made the sign of the cross. Indy closed his eyes and rested his head against the cool stone, summoning the strength to climb the passage.

"Bernabé," he said, tugging at his wallet. "You may have your bonus now."

The mist that earlier covered the lost city of Cozán had burned away by the time Indy and Bernabé emerged from the base of the pyramid. The sunlight reflecting from the chalky-white walls of the city stabbed at their eyes. Indy put a hand over his face, waiting for his pupils to adjust. When he could see clearly again he began brushing the dust and cobwebs from his clothes.

"Listen," Bernabé said.

Indy stopped brushing.

A low-pitched rumble came from the south.

"What is it?" Bernabé asked.

The sound grew louder.

"Engine noise," Indy said. "From an airplane."

The throaty beat of a pair of eight-hundred-horse-power engines filled the sky. Finally Indy caught a glimpse of white flashing beyond the trees to the south, the direction of the river.

"Look!" he said.

The aircraft popped into view over the city, and the shadow it cast engulfed the temple. The brilliant white craft looked like nothing Indy had seen before; its dominant feature was a huge boomeranglike wing with twin hulls slung beneath. Each hull had a row of round portholes down the side, and from the prow of each cabin jutted a machine-gun turret. Its broad tail was supported by booms extending from the rear of each hull, and the rudders were emblazoned with a trio of red stars, on a white field, within a green circle.

It was more than a flying boat, Indy thought; it was a colossal flying *catamaran.* The wingspan, he judged, had to be close to the length of a football field. The two massive engines were installed back-to-back above the center of the wing, on a tripodlike support, with one three-bladed propeller pushing and the other pulling. Through the rectangular windows of a raised cockpit in the center of the wing Indy could see the pilot and co-pilot, dressed in the same gray uniform with black piping that Marco had worn. The plane was low enough that Indy could tell Sarducci was leaning between them, a hand on each of their shoulders, laughing.

"Get down!" Indy shouted.

The guns in the nose turrets began to chatter.

Indy shoved Bernabé and jumped the other way. The Guatemalan guide went sprawling as bullets pocked the flagstones between them. Stone chips stung Indy's cheek and a ricochet passed so near that his entire body seemed to vibrate with the sound of its curious whine. Indy gritted his teeth and, with both hands, clamped his fedora down tightly on his head.

The guns stopped.

The roar of the engines receded.

Indy peeked from under the brim of his hat. Sunlight glinted from the starboard portholes as the flying boat began a long, slow turn.

Indy scrambled to his feet and pulled Bernabé up by the shirt collar. "This is our chance," he said. "We've got to disappear before they get lined up to make another pass."

The pair raced across the courtyard, dodging like quarterbacks the loose stones and debris in their path. Then they dashed down the Street of the Dead, the shortest path to the protection of the trees.

At the edge of the rain forest Indy paused and looked back at the flying boat, which had completed its turn and was now approaching from the east. His chest heaved and sweat dripped from his face. His cheek burned where the sweat and blood had mixed, and he rubbed it with the back of his hand.

"Who *are* those guys?" he asked.

"Nobody we want to know, boss."

They disappeared into the jungle.

The machine gunners strafed the patch of rain forest where they had last seen the fleeing pair. But Indy and Bernabé were crouched behind a mahogany tree a dozen yards away, listening as the bullets zipped impotently through the canopy of leaves overhead.

It was Thursday of Holy Week by the time they returned to San Pablo, far across the border in Guatemala. Rarely

had Indy been so tired—or so dirty. His clothes felt like
they were glued to his skin. He ached for a shower, a
shave, and a hot meal. As they neared town Indy paused,
shifted the weight of his pack, and scratched a mosquito
bite on his right hip. Then he continued on rubber legs.

Bernabé kept the same methodical pace he had
used since leaving San Pablo. The Indians of the area
were well-known for their stamina, and at each stage of
the journey Indy had used the sweep second hand of his
wristwatch to time Bernabé's barefoot steps. He discovered that Bernabé's pace did not vary by more than two
beats per minute. It had seemed remarkable at the beginning of the journey and strangely comforting in the
middle, but for the last few days Indy had found Bernabé's measured stride annoying; he irrationally began
to wish that Bernabé would run, or skip, or drag his feet.

"Come on," Indy urged. "We're almost there. Let's
run."

Bernabé smiled, but shook his head.

"Why not?" Indy asked.

"You remind me of the rabbit in that old story, boss.
Sometimes it's best to be the rabbit, other times it is
good to be the turtle. But we both get where we're going, no?"

"Well, according to the fable, the tortoise wins the
race."

"You don't say," Bernabé exclaimed, feigning surprise at this bit of news. "I'll have to remember that."

The pair entered San Pablo and made their way
through the dark, winding streets. The village consisted
of a handful of stucco buildings clustered around an aging colonial church. The town had no electricity, but the

plaza was ablaze with paper lanterns and fireworks. The air was filled with music and drunken laughter.

As they crossed the plaza their path was blocked by a procession of revelers. Some were portraying Roman soldiers, and the soldiers were dragging a villager Jesus to a wooden cage in the center of the plaza. Others, wearing felt hats and dark jackets, brandished bullwhips. The whips popped and cracked over the heads of the crowd.

"The ones with the whips are Judas," Bernabé said. "They are members of a brotherhood. The villagers give them whiskey and a little money to bring success in business for the coming year."

The crowd jeered as Jesus was forced into the wooden cage.

"But," Indy protested, "Judas . . ."

Bernabé shrugged.

"Christian things get a little confused with the old beliefs here," he said. "The priests don't like it. But what can they do? For my people, Judas is also Maximón, the Mayan god of the underworld who keeps the world turning by making people fall in love."

Something tugged at Indy's whip, which was coiled at his belt. He turned and found himself staring down into the frightened brown eyes of a child. She dropped a coin at his feet and ran.

Indy looked bewildered.

"She thought you were Judas," Bernabé said.

Indy crouched and picked up the coin. He held it between his thumb and forefinger and carefully examined it. It was a copper centavo, worth only a fraction of a U.S. cent. It had been minted in 1899, the year Indy was born.

He slipped the coin into his shirt pocket and stood.

"Bernabé," he said. "Tell me truly. What is the curse of the Crystal Skull?"

"Don't you know, boss?" Bernabé asked. "You will kill what you love."

1

BITS OF TRASH AND BONE

"What do you know of the Voynich Manuscript?"

Marcus Brody had asked the question while casually stirring cream and sugar into his coffee, but Indiana Jones had heard the tone—and had seen the sparkle in his old friend's eyes—before.

"Not much," Indy said, folding the morning edition of *The New York Times* and laying the newspaper aside. They were sitting at a sidewalk table beneath a canopy at the Tiger Coffee House on the corner of Nassau and Witherspoon, across the street from the Princeton University campus.

It was raining.

"As I recall, the manuscript is on loan at the rare book collection at Yale," Indy began, then took a sip from his mug of hot black coffee. "It is at least four hundred years old, was written in an unknown language by the alchemist Roger Bacon, and is reputed to hold the secret of the philosopher's stone—which, according to legend, has the power to turn lead into gold and to grant immortality. Its discovery created an international sensation a few years back, when I was a graduate student—it was called 'the world's most mysterious manuscript,' as I recall, but all attempts to decipher it have failed."

"Right as rain," Brody said, allowing himself a small smile. "I examined it once, more out of curiosity than anything else, but I couldn't make heads nor tails out of it. Don't think anyone could, not without the proper key."

"Why do you ask?"

"It's been stolen."

"It hasn't been reported in the papers."

"No, and I doubt that it will be," Brody said. "I learned of the theft just a few days ago when a pair of very serious government men visited me at the museum. And they asked quite a lot of questions about you."

"About me?"

"Yes," Brody said. "The university had told them you were away on a field expedition for the museum, and they wanted to know how to get in touch with you. Of course, I couldn't help them, since the Maya neglected to leave so much as a single public telephone in their ruins. Also, I didn't know when you would be back."

"I'm lucky to be back at all," Indy said.

For two years, since Brody had been named director of special acquisitions for the American Museum of Natural History in New York, the institution had quietly funded Indy's "research." The arrangement had enriched the museum's collection while allowing Indy the freedom to travel, which was a luxury not afforded by the salary of a university professor during the Great Depression.

Indy tugged absently at the necktie peeking above the collar of his sweater vest and stared at the cold spring rain lashing across Nassau Street in waves. An old woman was standing alone at curbside, selling apples from a wooden cart, her gray hair plastered to her head. Indy felt a growing sense of appreciation—and a momentary sense of guilt—for his dry seat, the warm coffee, and Brody's friendship.

"More coffee, Dr. Jones?"

"Pardon me?"

"Sir, would you care for more coffee?" the waiter asked.

"I'm sorry. I was someplace else for a moment," Indy said. "No thank you. I have class soon."

Brody held up his hand, and the waiter passed.

"You say your visitors were government men?" Indy asked. "It makes me wonder why the FBI would be interested in the theft of something so unusual. Also, who would want to steal such a thing in the first place?"

"A private collector would be my first guess," Brody said. "That may be why they want to talk to you, to see if you could provide them with any leads."

"That's more your area than mine."

"Perhaps they want you to help them recover it," Brody said, and the sparkle was back. "If anybody can do it, you can."

"Not interested," Indy said. "I need a rest."

From his leather briefcase, Indy withdrew a sheaf of handwritten papers. "Here is the report on the Cozán expedition," he said. He had already briefed Brody ear-

lier that morning about the loss of the Crystal Skull, but
had carefully avoided any mention of the curse that Bernabé said it carried. "I'm sorry the story doesn't have a
happier ending. I don't even know who those guys in
the airplane were. I feel bad for wasting the museum's
money by returning empty-handed."

Brody brushed the apology aside with a wave of his
hand.

"Archaeology is not an exact science," he gently
reminded Indy. "Every venture into the unknown car-
ries with it an element of risk. The finds you have already made for us far outweigh any minor setback, and I
am disappointed only because you are."

Indy shook his head.

"Sometimes I wonder what all of these dead bits of
trash and bone really amount to in the scheme of
things," Indy said. "There are so many hungry people in
the world. I doubt that the woman selling apples there
cares in the least for what happened a thousand years
ago, or even yesterday. Yesterday, at least, the sun was
shining."

"I worry about you when you become philosophic,"
Brody said. "We each have our part to play. It is true
that too many of us are occupied right now with filling
our stomachs. But you, my boy—the part you play with
your bits of trash and bone helps to fill our souls. And
who knows? You may one day discover an ancient secret
that could help fill our stomachs as well."

Marcus leaned forward.

"The more we learn about the past, Indy, the less
we are doomed to repeat it."

The rain slowed and finally dwindled to a few big
drops breaking the surface of the puddles in the street.

Indy reached out and cupped some of the water dripping from the edge of the white-and-green-striped canopy. He held the rainwater in his palm for a moment, then closed his hand, and the moisture seeped between his fingers.

"What's gotten into you, Indy?" Marcus asked. "I've never seen you so dispirited before. Do I need to recite your list of accomplishments?

"No, Marcus," he said. "I'm fine, really."

"Did something happen that you're not telling me about?" Marcus asked. "An affair of the heart. You met a beautiful Indian girl who—"

"Nothing like that," Indy said, brightening. "The only female I met on this trip was made of quartz and was a few dozen centuries too old for me." He finished his coffee and glanced at the sky. "It's been good to see you, Marcus, but I'd better make a run for it while I can."

"The coffee is on me," Brody said.

"Thanks," Indy said. "For everything."

"Won't you consider coming to New York to view the opening of the new Central American exhibit?" Brody asked. "It would do you good. It is really quite something to see, and as you know, you are responsible for the best pieces. Besides, it would be a good opportunity to introduce you to the Explorers' Club."

"Thanks, but no," Indy said. "I haven't even unpacked my bags yet. I just got out of one jungle, and I'm not anxious to plunge into another."

Indy donned his hat and slipped his leather case beneath his arm. The two men shook hands.

"I'll be in touch," Brody said. When Indy had left

the coffee shop, Brody said to himself: "My boy, I hope she was worth it."

At the corner, Indy paused to buy an apple. He paid with a dollar bill, and when the woman protested that she didn't have ninety-five cents in change, he asked her to keep the money for something hot to eat.

Indy slipped the apple into his case while watching a new V-8 Ford pass, its tires singing on the wet pavement. The car was black, and the two men in the front seat wore dark suits and ties. A third man, in the back, was in uniform. The license plate on the rear fender identified the vehicle as government property.

Indy crossed to the Fitz Randolph Gateway. The wrought-iron gate was opened only on special occasions, and Indy had to pass through the smaller side entrance ordinarily used by students. He had made it halfway across the campus, and was abreast of the big cannon left over from the Revolutionary War, when the gray skies rumbled and began to pour again. By the time he reached the steps of McCormick Hall, Indy was soaked.

"All wet again, eh, Jones?"

"Gruber," Indy said.

Harold Gruber—a pipe-smoking medievalist with a passion for Machiavelli—was acting chairman of the Department of Art and Architecture at Princeton University.

Gruber took the briar from the corner of his mouth.

"Look here, Jones," he said, pointing the stem of his pipe at Indy. "You really ought to get an umbrella. There's no excuse for being unprepared."

"Thanks, Harry," Indy said.

"Harold," Gruber said.

Indy started up the stairs, his wet shoes squishing

with every step. Gruber and his smoldering pipe followed.

"I'm rather glad I caught you," Gruber mumbled, the pipe again in the corner of his mouth. "There have been questions, you know, and as acting chair, I feel it is my duty to respond to them."

"Questions?" Indy asked over his shoulder.

"Um, yes," Gruber said. They had reached the top floor now, and Indy was leaving a trail of wet footprints as he marched to his office at the end of the hall. "We have a complaint from the British consulate about your activities in British Honduras. It seems they feel you trumped their antiquities law by reaching some sites in the interior by way of Guatemala—taking the back door, it would seem."

"The back door?" Indy asked.

Indy unlocked the door to 404E and slipped inside. A pile of messages had accumulated beneath the door, and he knelt to scoop them up.

"Well?" Gruber demanded.

A column of angry smoke rose from the briar. The tobacco was an especially foul shag mixture and it made Indy's eyes burn.

"I don't remember any back doors." Indy stood and shuffled through the messages as he spoke. "But I am notoriously bad about reading maps. I'll have to write my Guatemalan guide and ask him where exactly we were. Of course, Harry, it will take a few weeks to receive a reply. . . ."

Indy shut the door and locked it.

"Harold," Gruber said from the other side of the door. "I prefer Harold."

Indy hung his dripping hat and overcoat on the top

rung of a wooden coatrack in the corner of his small
office, then placed the leather case on his desk. The
office had been locked up since Easter vacation began,
and it smelled as musty as a tomb. Indy turned, slipped
the latch on the window, and opened the bottom pane a
few inches.

A breeze flowed in, ruffling the papers on the desk.
Indy savored the aroma of rainwashed spring air. He sat
down in the swivel chair behind the desk, removed his
wet wing tips, and placed them upside down on top of
the hissing steam radiator beneath the window.

The office was littered with books, scholarly journals, and an incongruous mix of artifacts. A human skull
from the temple of Angkor Wat grinned down at Indy
from the top of an overflowing bookcase. A plaster cast
of the Rosetta Stone occupied one corner behind his
desk, while a fierce wooden fetish from Polynesia stood
guard in the other. Boxes were scattered everywhere,
containing collections of arrow and spear points, shards
of pottery, assorted fossils. On the desk was a telephone,
an inkwell, a pile of ungraded papers, and a ceremonial
dish from the grave of an Egyptian king.

Indy put on his reading glasses. He opened the
leather case and began searching for the notes to the
morning's lecture. Finding none, he rummaged the top
drawer of his desk. He was scouring the bottom drawer
when there came a thudding knock at his office door.

"Go away, Harold," Indy said.

The knock persisted.

"Dr. Jones?" a voice called.

Indy muttered under his breath. He glanced across
the desktop and peered at the floor beneath, before rising from his chair to unlock the door.

The three men from the V-8 Ford were waiting on the other side. The pair in front wore dark suits, while the man standing behind wore an army officer's uniform.

"Indiana Jones?"

"Yes," Indy said impatiently.

"Sorry to both—" the beefy man in front started to say, then stopped when he saw that Indy was patting himself down in an attempt to locate the missing cards. "Is anything the matter?"

"What? Oh," Indy said, and grinned foolishly. "I have misplaced my lecture notes for this morning. Please excuse my absentmindedness."

"Well, I suppose it goes with the territory," the beefy man said, suspiciously eyeing Indy's argyle socks. "Do you mind if we come in?"

The bell in the cupola atop Nassau Hall began to toll, a sharpened D note summoning students to class.

"I haven't much time," Indy said.

"Neither have we," the man said. "This is a matter of some importance, and we have come all the way from Washington to see you. Surely you can spare us a few minutes."

Indy glanced at his wristwatch.

"Why not?" he said.

The trio squeezed into the office while Indy moved boxes from chairs to make room for them to sit. Then he returned to his desk and picked up the telephone receiver.

"Some urgent business just dropped by," he told Penelope Angstrom, the department secretary. "Would you be kind enough to inform my nine o'clock students? Yes. I will be there shortly. Oh, and Miss Angstrom? Ask them to review the material on Troy. Thank you."

Indy replaced the receiver.

"I am Agent Bieber," the muscular man said, extending his hand. "My partner's name is Yartz. We're with the FBI. This is our consultant, Major John M. Manly."

Indy shook hands with all three. Yartz was a lean, pleasant-looking man. Manly was older than both of them, with a strong jaw and clear brown eyes.

"I know of your work, Major," Indy said. "I was impressed with your criticism of Newbold's solution in the *Speculum*. But tell me, if you would, how the country's best Chaucer scholar was recruited by army intelligence?"

Manly smiled.

"I have a talent for puzzles," Manly said. "I was recruited by the cryptographic corps just before America entered the Great War, and still render it some small service in the hope of avoiding the next. Say, I believe I met your father, Henry Jones, when I was at the University of Chicago before the war. He was teaching here at Princeton then. How is the old man?"

"Dad and I haven't seen each other in years."

Bieber lit a Lucky Strike and offered the pack to Indy.

"I don't smoke," Indy said.

Bieber shrugged as he picked a fleck of tobacco from his lower lip. He passed the cigarettes to Yartz.

"Gentlemen, let me save you some time," Indy said, and removed his glasses. "My colleague Marcus Brody told me to expect you. I'm afraid that I can't help you with the Voynich Manuscript because crime is just not my field. What you see around you, these things that are taken from the earth, is what I'm good at. You have your expert in Professor Manly."

"Let's not jump ahead of ourselves," Bieber said, smiling through a cloud of blue smoke. He took a pencil and a dimestore pad from his pocket. "We would like to begin with you, Dr. Jones. Can you explain your interest in the occult?"

"I beg your pardon?"

"I'm told that you have carved a niche for yourself in some of the darker corners of archaeology. Witches, black magic, even human sacrifice. You're known as something of an expert. To a normal person, this would seem rather . . . unhealthy."

Indy laughed.

"The matter is really quite simple. To ancient cultures, magic was real. It was an everyday part of their world. It told them when to hunt, when to plant, when to build cities. Any serious study of those cultures requires an understanding of those beliefs—it doesn't mean I practice them."

Bieber grunted.

"What about your connection with this museum in New York?" he asked. "It seems there have been various complaints about your shadowy archaeological digs. Your conduct, we are told, couldn't exactly be called exemplary. The British consulate is hopping mad over your last escapade."

"You've been talking to Gruber, haven't you?" Indy asked.

"Perhaps it's something that bears checking into," Bieber said. The ash on his cigarette had grown dangerously long, and he flicked it into the ceremonial dish on Indy's desk.

Indy grimaced and brushed the ashes away.

"Please use the ashtray on the shelf behind you," he said, "instead of this three-thousand-year-old Egyptian artifact."

"Sorry," Bieber muttered.

"I apologize for my companion's heavy-handed-ness," Yartz said, smiling broadly. "He often uses a bull-dozer when a garden spade would do. What we are trying to get at, Dr. Jones, is that the agency might be willing to overlook—well, some of your past transgres-sions—if you could lend us a hand with the Voynich case."

"Why me?" Indy asked.

"Your reputation precedes you," Yartz said. "It is our understanding that your unconventional methods can be rather successful. It is not so much that we want to solve this crime, but that we want the manuscript recovered, by any means necessary."

"By any means necessary?" Indy asked. "This just doesn't add up. Why is the government so keenly inter-ested in the return of an ancient, unreadable manu-script?"

The agents were silent.

Major Manly held his hands palm-up.

"I'm sorry, Dr. Jones," he said. "This is an FBI operation, at least within the boundaries of the United States. At army intelligence, we operate on a more global scale."

Bieber frowned.

"Look here, Dr. Jones," he said. "Be reasonable. You have nothing to gain by being difficult. You have a reputation as a good teacher—that's what your students report—and it would be unfortunate if anything happened to soil your record."

"Is that a threat?" Indy asked.

"We don't make threats, Dr. Jones," Bieber said.

"Gentlemen, I don't like being pressured," Indy said. "If you'll excuse me, I have a class to teach. You know the way out."

Bieber dropped his cigarette butt and ground it out with his heel. Yartz smiled, took a stack of note cards from his jacket, and placed them on Indy's desk.

"You dropped these when you crossed the street," Yartz said.

The FBI agents walked out.

Manly lingered behind.

"From one scholar to another," he said, "this is a matter of some importance. I apologize for the obtuseness of my colleagues. Frankly, Dr. Jones, we could use your help. We haven't a single lead that has developed into anything substantial. At least give this some thought."

Indy was silent.

"Here is my card," Manly said. When Indy made no move to take it, he placed the card on the desk. "You can reach me at this number, any time of the day or night."

Manly closed the door behind him.

Notes in hand, Indy paused at the classroom door. The room was buzzing with the joking and idle conversation of fifteen students who suddenly found themselves with a few unexpected minutes on their hands. He smiled and opened the door.

The classroom fell abruptly silent.

"Gentlemen," Indy said. "I apologize for the delay. I hope you all had a pleasant—if too brief—vacation. But let us resume our exploration of the connection between myth and discovery."

Indy went to the board.

"The story of archaeology is the story of our elusive quest for the past," he said. "Each of us, every day, walks about with the cultural furniture of our long-dead ancestors stored in the dark basement of our unconscious.

"For most of us, those echoes are merely a footnote to everyday life. Even if we don't believe in superstition, for example, most of us find it difficult to cross the path of a black cat without feeling at least a twinge of doubt. That bit of superstition comes to us from the Babylonians. But there are other, more intriguing items that clutter the basements of our heads: stories, fables, myth."

Indy wrote a name on the board: SCHLIEMAN.

"For a few people these myths sometimes take on the driving force of passion, and it becomes their life's work to solve the mysteries surrounding them. It is, in fact, surprising to note how many discoveries in the history of archaeology have been made by a few inspired individuals operating on little more than belief and hard work."

A hand went up in front.

"Yes, Mr. Hudson?"

"Ah, excuse me, Dr. Jones," the sophomore said, twisting his pencil nervously in his hands. "I believe Schliemann is spelled with two *n*'s—that is, if I'm not mistaken."

"Absolutely," Indy said, correcting his mistake.

"Thank you. And please, feel free to contribute in my classroom. You needn't hesitate."

Hudson nodded.

"Now, in Christmas 1829, a seven-year-old boy's father gave his son a picture book depicting the history of the world. In that book was a drawing of the burning of Troy. The picture, which showed the city's massive walls and the legendary Scæen Gate, excited the boy's imagination. He listened with rapt attention as his father recounted the story of the Trojan War, and was astonished when he was told the city had vanished—that nobody alive knew where the great citadel had stood. The boy resolved that when he was grown, he would find Troy and the treasure it contained.

"The boy—Heinrich Schliemann—grew up. His formal schooling ended at fourteen, but he continued to study on his own. While working as a grocer's apprentice, a cabin boy, and a bookkeeper, he managed to master eight languages. He eventually became a very successful businessman, but he never lost his obsession with Troy.

"Finally, at age forty-six, at the height of his success, he retired from business to pursue his quest. To guide him, he had nothing more than Homer's account of the Trojan War—which most scholars regarded as a fairy tale. But Schliemann preferred the pick and shovel to the opinion of others. In 1873, after years of digging —and on the day after he had vowed to abandon the work for lack of success—he unearthed the treasure trove of a king.

"More spectacular finds were to follow," Indy said. "It was estimated at the time that all of the world's museums did not hold one fifth as much treasure as the golden artifacts that Schliemann discovered at Troy. Now, who can place Schliemann's find in an archaeological context for us? Mr. York."

"The Troy that Schliemann found probably was not the Troy of Homeric myth," a young redheaded man said confidently. "In the 1890s, Wilhelm Dorpfeld was the first to realize that there were nine cities, each built atop the ruins of the one before it, at the site."

Another hand went up.

"Hudson."

"Last year," the timid scholar ventured, "Carl Blegen—of the University of Cincinnati, I think—began a new research expedition. It is his belief, however, that one of the nine cities at the location probably is the *real* Troy."

"Very good," Indy said. "So, although Schliemann made some mistakes—and was scorned by the experts at the time as a meddlesome outsider—he discovered a three-thousand-year-old civilization that most scholars once thought resided only in myth. It was the realization of a dream born in the heart of a seven-year-old boy. Now, before we get into the stratification at Troy, are there questions or comments thus far?"

A student in the back row lifted an index finger.

"Mr. Griffith?"

"Where," the young man asked, "are your shoes?"

Miss Penelope Angstrom was fifty-six years old and had devoted herself to the Department of Art and Architecture at Princeton University for the last twenty-nine years. Although she bristled at suggestions that she was married to the department, she secretly fretted about becoming an old maid. She lived alone in a two-room apartment above a five-and-dime on Witherspoon Street, overlooking Palmer Square, but was seldom lonely, because she had her books and her music to keep her company. When she *was* lonely she read poetry or gently played her violin until late into the night or, if she were feeling particularly daring, would gorge on adventure novels from the corner newsstand.

It wasn't that she had never had suitors, but that none of them had ever measured up to her standards. She had had a lover, in the summer of her thirtieth year, but he had taken her money along with her innocence. Although she confided it to no one, and felt foolish even admitting it to herself, she wanted a man of pure heart who was ready to fight for what was good in the world—in short, a modern knight. And, she wanted a love poem written just for her. But now that a touch of winter had appeared in her dark brown hair, her hope had dimmed. Her sonnet seemed far away indeed. If only, she thought wistfully, she could be twenty once again—things were so different for girls now. She had watched a generation of women bob their hair, drink bathtub gin, and not wait for heroes to come to *them.*

Penelope Angstrom was dwelling upon these things at her desk in front of the chairman's office at the end of the hall when Indy tapped lightly on the open door. He startled her so that she dropped the pencil she had been holding and it rolled across the floor to Indy.

"Daydreaming, Miss Angstrom?" he asked, returning the pencil.

"Certainly not," she said. "I was making a mental list of the afternoon's activities. It helps to collect one's thoughts occasionally, Dr. Jones."

"I had a note that Harold wanted to see me," Indy said.

"Of course." She spoke briefly into the intercom. "Dr. Gruber will be with you shortly. Please take a seat."

Indy sat in one of the stiff wooden chairs lining one wall of the office, the chairs where students usually waited in various states of anxiety.

"I hope your trip to Central America was productive," she said, softening a bit.

"Not as productive as I was hoping," Indy said. "But thank you for asking. Speaking of travel, has there been any word from Dr. Morey?"

"Yes, I received a postcard from him yesterday. He reports that he is keeping himself busy at the Vatican, but he says he misses Princeton badly and is looking forward to his return in the fall." She leaned forward conspiratorially. "Between you and me, Dr. Jones, I cannot wait until he's back. I've spent much of my time lately cleaning up the messes that Dr. Gruber has made."

"Harry does seem to have a talent for it," Indy said. "And just between us, Miss Angstrom, I know how much the department owes to you—why, I doubt if we could survive a week without you."

She blushed.

"Thank you," she stammered.

She hesitated, then said: "I may be out of line for saying this, Dr. Jones, but I have truly enjoyed having you with us. I know, too, that you are one of Dr. Morey's favorites among the younger faculty, and I believe his faith is well placed. You are unlike so many of the others. Why is it that when a man gets a few letters after his name he turns into an egotistical snob who treats students like so much cattle? But you and Dr. Morey both have managed to retain . . . well, your humanity."

It was Indy's turn to blush.

"Dr. Jones," she said suddenly, "I *was* daydreaming when you came in. I was thinking about time, and how strange it is to be growing old when inside I still feel like a schoolgirl. This may sound like an odd question, but do you think there really could be a fountain of youth somewhere?"

"It's a universal myth," Indy said. "People have spent their lives searching for it. Ponce de León thought it was in Florida, and the Indians in Central America believed in a magical spring in the Bahamas."

The intercom buzzed.

"Dr. Gruber will see you now," she said.

Harold Gruber did not acknowledge Indy's presence when he entered the chairman's office. Indy stood while Gruber sat in Rufus Morey's big swivel chair and studied a typewritten document in his hands. Finally he looked up and slid the paper across to Indy.

"That's a letter of resignation, ready for your signature," Gruber said, placing his hands behind his head.

"May I ask for what reason?"

"Don't play games with me," Gruber said, and leaned forward. "You know very well. You violated the law when you went to British Honduras in your search for black-market treasure."

"Black market?" Indy asked. "I was on an expedition for the museum. Call Marcus Brody in New York—he will clear this up."

"Ah, the museum front. Is Brody your confederate

in this operation?" Gruber asked. "The gentlemen that were here this morning gave me a full report. It seems they've been keeping their eyes on you for some time. It would be in the university's best interest for you to move on."

"This is blackmail," Jones said. "The men you talked to this morning—"

Gruber held up his hand.

"I won't tolerate your lies," he said. "If you can't trust the FBI, then who can you trust? You have until the end of the day to clear your things out of 404E, or we'll have you thrown out."

Indy rubbed his jaw in thought.

"What about my classes?"

"We have a competent faculty ready to take up the slack."

"Has Dr. Morey been contacted?"

"No need," Gruber said smugly. "I conferred with President Dodd this morning, and he agreed with my assessment of the situation. Actually, Jones, I'm doing you a favor by giving you the option of resigning."

"Some favor."

"The letter I've prepared for you cites 'personal reasons' for your leaving. You would be wise to sign it— otherwise, you'll never teach again."

"I won't resign," Indy said, "because I've done nothing wrong. Harry, if you want to get rid of me, then you're going to have to fire me." He tore the letter of resignation into pieces.

"Jones," Gruber said, "you're fired."

2

THE MOST MYSTERIOUS MANUSCRIPT

Indiana Jones paused at the top of the double stone staircase leading to the main entrance of the American Museum of Natural History. The sun, about to dip below the city skyline, cast long shadows over 77th Street; to the east, it painted the trees in Central Park with a bucolic glow. Rush hour was over, and the raucous ragtime of taxis and pedestrians with not a minute to spare had diminished. Inspired by the uncharacteristic near quiet, Indy wondered if a few thousand years hence a future archaeologist might not stand atop the same staircase, survey the remains of the city, and speculate on what manner of people had once lived here.

His reverie was broken by the squeal of tires as a pair of taxis skidded to a near miss on the street below. One of the drivers laid on his horn while the offending driver, with perfect confidence, extended his arm and gave the universal hand signal of ultimate disrespect.

Indy shook his head and entered the museum.

He skirted the reptile display, which occupied the center of the first hall, but he felt the cold glass eyes of a stuffed anaconda staring at him from an all-too-realistic jungle setting. He hurried to the east stairwell, where the elevator was located in one corner, and entered the cage with some relief.

"Floor?" the operator asked.

"Fifth."

"No exhibits above the fourth floor, mister," the man said, straightening the jacket of his uniform. "Administrative offices, laboratories, and library. No tourists."

"Who's a tourist? I'm Professor—I mean, Dr. Jones. I'm here to see Marcus Brody." He paused, then softened. "I collected many of the artifacts in the new Central American exhibit."

The operator pulled back the brass lever. The elevator glided upward while the man looked to the front with a practiced expression of disinterest.

"Perhaps you've heard of me," Indy said hopefully.

The man glanced over and gave Indy the once-over, from his wing tips to his bow tie.

"Nope," he said. "Brody, I know. You, I never heard of."

Indy stepped off the elevator feeling somewhat smaller. He should have known better, he told himself, than to attempt to bolster his sagging ego by seeking the approval of a stranger. But in the days since he'd lost his position at Princeton, his confidence had slowly eroded. At least, Indy thought, the man had been honest.

.   .   .

Indy and Marcus Brody took the stairs down. They paused only once, at the southwest wing of the second floor, to take a quick look at the *Archaeology of Mexico and Central America* exhibit. The center of the room was dominated by cast reproductions of ceremonial stones, stelæ, and frescoes. THE ORNAMENTS OF GOLD, JADE, AND PRECIOUS STONES BEFORE YOU, informed a placard on a glass case in the center of the room, WERE DISCOVERED BY DR. HENRY JONES, JR. OF PRINCETON UNIVERSITY IN A COMPLEX OF ANCIENT GRAVES IN COSTA RICA. OF PARTICULAR NOTE ARE THE RELIGIOUS EMBLEMS OF FANTASTIC DESIGN INCLUDING CROCODILE SWALLOWING A SNAKE, BIRDLIKE FIGURE WITH LIZARD, AND MAN DEVOURED BY VULTURE. Other cases contained pottery and earthenware from a variety of periods. Site maps showed the location of the cities, wells, and graves. A curious reclining figure—a plaster copy of the real one at Chichén Itzá—presided over the exhibit with an inscrutable smile.

"You've done a fine job, Marcus," Indy said.

"You deserve the thanks," Brody said. "This is the result of your hard work. Your field notes were exceptional, and it was a simple matter to arrange the artifacts in a comprehensible fashion. Of course, I had hoped the Crystal Skull would be the centerpiece."

"She may be yet," Indy said.

"She?" Brody asked.

"Sorry," Indy said, feeling foolish. "Something I picked up from Sarducci—whoever he was. By the way, have you had any luck connecting the name with any bald-headed men?"

"Not in the least," Brody said. "Neither the name nor the description has rung any bells with my colleagues. Of course, I will continue my inquiries."

"Discreetly, I hope," Indy said. "Whoever these people were, they had a liking for firepower."

The pair left the museum. It was a pleasant evening and they strolled south, past the blocks of hotels that stood like sentinels along Central Park West. At the Majestic, on the corner of 72nd Street, a cab pulled to the curb. A man emerged whose beard, cane, and dark suit would have been more at home, Indy thought, in the Victorian era.

"Brody," the man said warmly. "Where have you been hiding? We missed you at the last meeting. Chapman began telling his war stories about that damned expedition to the Gobi, and I don't see why *you* should have been spared."

"I'm afraid my work has kept me away," Brody said. "But I'm glad we chanced upon each other, because there is someone I want you to meet—someone, I daresay, who would be an excellent addition to the club."

"Please continue," the man said.

"Indy, this is Vilhjalmur Stefansson, president of the famed Explorers' Club. It meets upstairs, here at the Majestic."

Stefansson offered his hand.

"President Stefansson," Brody said, "may I present the noted scholar-adventurer, Indiana Jones."

"Indiana Jones!"

Stefansson's hand stopped in midshake.

"Good Lord, man, I've recently heard of some of your adventures from the other members," he said.

"I'm sure they exaggerate," Indy said modestly. A gratifying warmth had begun to spread across his chest.

"No, you don't understand," Stefansson said, withdrawing his hand. "Adventures are a mark of incompetence! Certainly nothing to brag about. And your methods—oh, the horror! Brody, why are you wasting my time with this man?"

Indy's glow turned to ice water in his chest.

"I beg your pardon," Brody said. "Dr. Jones is very well regarded—"

"Pshaw!" Stefansson said, and shook his cane at Indy. "You, sir, are nothing but a grave robber! A common thief has more decency. Step aside."

"Now, see here—"

"No more from you, Brody. One is judged by the company he keeps, and I suggest that in the future you consider yours more carefully."

Stefansson passed between them. He entered the hotel without a backward glance.

Indy thrust his hands in his pockets and sighed.

"Well," Brody said, patting Indy on the shoulder. "It's their loss. What would you say to a nice dinner and a spot of wine? Nothing picks up the spirits like a good meal. I know a marvelous Italian restaurant not far from here."

"I hope you're buying," Indy said.

On the sidewalk in front of Carmine's, Indy thanked Marcus Brody for dinner and remarked that he felt better, although Brody should have warned him about the garlic. Brody laughed and observed that Indy did look better, although to himself he allowed it may have been from the reddish glow of the restaurant's neon light.

"Where are you staying?" Brody inquired. "You are welcome to take up digs with me while you're here in the city."

"Thanks, but I'm afraid I would just be underfoot,"

Indy said. "You've worried enough about my health as it
is. I think I'll take a stroll downtown and look for a quiet
room where I can pass a day or two and organize myself.
Study the *Times* want ads, polish my résumé, that sort of
thing. Besides, I left my bags in a locker at Penn Station
when I arrived from New Jersey, and I need to pick
them up."

"Of course," Brody said. "But do keep in touch. If
you need anything"—and by this Indy knew that Brody
meant money—"by all means let me know. And, Indy—
I know things will soon turn around for you. This business at Princeton is nothing but a misunderstanding."

Indy offered his hand.

Brody reached to grasp it, and Indy drew him into a
bear hug.

"My word," Brody said when Indy had released
him. His face had turned a few shades redder than even
the neon sign could make it. "No need to be overly
sentimental."

"No need," Indy agreed.

Brody stepped off the curb and hailed a cab. He
waved as the automobile pulled away. Indy pulled his
leather jacket tight against the evening chill, adjusted
his fedora, and turned south.

Indy didn't know where he was going, but he felt a
need to walk. As the street numbers dwindled from the
sixties to the fifties, and then into the forties, he left
the posh hotels and restaurants behind and entered the
working districts. Canyons of drab brick buildings with
family shops on the first floors rose on either side, punc-
tuated occasionally by the elevated railway overhead.
The city grew darker, except for the beacons provided
by the lighted twenty-four-hour missions and soup

kitchens and, on the corners, the ubiquitous flaming barrels with their grim-faced men in shabby clothes.

"Spare a dime for a veteran?" pleaded a one-legged man leaning on a crutch at the mouth of an alleyway. He had a British accent and his ragged coat suggested that he was once a member of His Majesty's army.

Indy had the urge to quicken his pace without acknowledging the man's presence, but he stopped and dug for change in his trouser pocket. He was terribly low on cash—his dismissal had not included any type of severance pay—but he fished a quarter from his pocket and placed it in the greasy palm.

"Here's wishing you better times," he said.

"Thank you, sir," the man said. His alcoholic breath was brutal.

"Spend it on a good meal," Indy suggested.

"My meals come in pints," the one-legged man said.

"Something of a liquid diet, then," Indy said with a smile.

"You have a sense of humor. That's good," the man said, and regarded Indy through bloodshot eyes. "Captain, if you don't mind my asking, what brings you to this part of town? It ain't exactly *safe,* you know."

"Just walking," Indy said.

"Oh, none of us ever just walk," the man said. "Not here."

"True enough," Indy said. "I'm looking for a room for the night. Actually, I just lost my job and I need to stretch my cash a bit."

"That's horrible," the man said.

"You can have pity for *me*?" Indy asked.

"Of course," the man said, and stiffened. "I may be a bum, but I'm not an animal."

"Sorry," Indy said. "And I don't think you're a bum."

"Oh, but I am—and you needn't feel badly for me. And if I were you, I'd keep a tight hold on the purse strings down here. You can't afford to feed every character that begs for it. As the Lord himself said, the poor will always be with us. I'm just doing my bloody job."

Indy smiled.

"Tommy Atkins, at your service," the man said, and nearly fell when he attempted a polite bow. "Lost that damn leg in the Argonne, haven't found it since."

"You can call me Jones," Indy said as he helped Atkins regain his balance. "Since you know this neighborhood so well, perhaps you could suggest a room for the night. Nothing fancy—just a bed and a chair and a little light."

"Ah, Captain. That's a tough one. We don't get many holiday vacationers down this way. But I believe there is a place, over on 36th Street. Above the grocery. The hen who runs it is as crusty as three-day-old bread, but she'll treat you right."

"Which direction would that be?"

"Lost, are we? Lucky you are that Tommy Atkins was here to help. Well, if you follow this alley for two blocks, take a right, and go four more blocks, then you'll be there. Sign in the window."

"Much obliged," Indy said.

"Mind your back," Atkins called as Indy walked away.

Indy walked briskly for two blocks down the alley, took a right, and walked four long east-west New York blocks before he found himself as lost as when he had started. There was no sign of any kind of grocery, just dark rows of buildings. He attempted to retrace his steps, but could not locate the alley from which he had emerged.

Embarrassment began to warm his shirt collar.

"This is ridiculous," he muttered. "I can pick my way in or out of any pyramid in the world—African or otherwise—but I can't follow directions for six city blocks."

He kept walking.

In the middle of the next block, in a building that looked as if it had been lifted from the pages of a Dickens novel, Indy found a shop with a light in the window. Inside, a monkish man was bent over a table intently studying a book that looked as if it were about to fall apart in his hands.

Indy glanced at the name above the front door: CAD-MAN'S RARE BOOKS, 611 W. 34TH ST. TELEPHONE BRYANT 5250. "A GOOD BOOK IS LIKE A GOOD FRIEND"—MARTIN TUP-PER. A hand-lettered sign in the front window announced: ROOMS.

Indy rapped on the front door.

The man was either so absorbed with his book that he didn't move, or he was trying to ignore Indy.

He knocked hard enough to rattle the glass.

With a look of disgust the man carefully marked his place in the book, gently laid it aside, and climbed down from his stool. He took a sip of cold tea from a cup on the table, then limped up the aisle to the door. He pointed to the CLOSED sign and shook his head.

"A room," Indy said, pointing at the sign. "I'd like a room."

The elevated train was rumbling by and the man couldn't hear him.

With an even sterner look of distaste the man unlocked the dead bolt and opened the door a crack. A chain lock still barred Indy's entrance.

"I told the others everything I knew," the man said.

"No, you don't understand—"

"We're closed. Come back tomorrow. Or never."

"But—"

"I have nothing more on Voynich," the man snapped.

Indy's foot shot into the doorjamb.

"Voynich?"

"Yes, Voynich," the man said. "Look, do you want me to call the police? Please leave me alone. You people are positively exhausting. Are you a moron or don't you understand plain English? We are *closed.* Remove your foot or I'll be forced to drop the *A* through *L* of the *Oxford Unabridged* upon it. It can break toes, you know."

"No, please," Indy said. "Forgive my manners. I am actually here to inquire about a room. Your sign," he reminded him.

"Oh," the man said. "It's rather late."

"That is why I'm so desperate."

"Where's your bag? I don't rent to strangers without luggage."

"I'm afraid I'm lost," Indy said.

"Lost?"

"Quite."

The man grunted.

"What do you do for a living?"

"I'm an archaeologist."

"And they send you out by yourself?"

"Never without a guide," Indy said.

The man opened the door.

"Two dollars for the night," he said. "The rooms are upstairs, the bathroom is down the hall. No breakfast. No smoking or drinking in the room. There's a stairwell that leads up to them. Step inside, and I'll get you a key."

"Thank you," Indy said.

The man locked the door behind them.

It was the most disordered shop that Indy had ever seen. Books were stacked everywhere, on the floor and on the tables, and in stacks in front of the already over-full shelves. A path led from the front door to a desk and a couple of chairs in the middle, and on toward the stairs in the back. A thick layer of dust covered it all and, combined with the musty smell of old and mildewed books, threatened to make Indy sneeze.

"My name's Cadman—Roger Cadman," the man said. "Don't let looks fool you. We do our business by mail. Collectors, mostly. Don't get many walk-ins. Had those two groups asking about that damned manuscript last week, and it almost drove me crazy. Considered painting the entire front of the store black, with just a number."

"The manuscript?" Indy asked. "Voynich?"

"Yes," the man said. "You know of it?"

Indy nodded.

"Voynich was a competitor of mine," Cadman said. "Those were the good old days, when we raced one another all over Europe fighting over crates of books that everyone else considered worthless. I'm too old for that now."

"You don't appear to be," Indy said.

"Maybe my heart just isn't in it anymore," Cadman agreed. "So many good things were destroyed in the war. Your money, please."

"What?"

"Two dollars."

Indy brought out his billfold and handed over the money. Cadman took a key from the desk drawer and placed it in Indy's palm.

"Number seven, at the end of the hall."

"Could you tell me a bit more about Voynich?" Indy asked. "I mean, if you wouldn't mind. The FBI came to me—"

"They were here as well," Cadman said. "Two very brusque fellows—"

"Bieber and Yartz?"

"Yes! They acted as if I were hiding something, and I told them all I knew. Then there were those Italian fellows in their curious uniforms."

Indy's throat tightened.

"Uniforms?"

"Gray, with black," Cadman said. "They really looked quite peculiar. Do you know them?"

"We've met," Indy said through clenched teeth.

"Left you with the same impression, I see. Told them that if they needed another book to burn, they should consider some of that awful stuff that Mussolini writes."

"The fascists have no sense of humor," Indy said. "Did they give you any names? Leave a card, perhaps, or an address or telephone number where they could be reached?"

"Nothing," Cadman said. "I didn't recognize the

uniforms, and I know they were Italian only because of
their accents. They certainly seemed to hate intellectuals," Cadman said. "Not that I consider myself one,
but—" He moved a stack of books from a wooden chair.

"Sit down," he said. "Would you like some tea? I
could make some fresh."

"That," Indy said, "would be terribly kind of you."
He felt a cautious hope growing within him.

Indy sat while Cadman placed a kettle on a hot
plate. When the water was boiling he poured each of
them a cup. Cadman used his old tea bag and gave Indy
a fresh one.

"Let me be straight with you," Indy told his host.
"My interest in Voynich is more than academic. The FBI
asked me to help them recover it, and I had a rather
unpleasant experience with these gray-suited fascists
that may be related."

"I suspected that it had been stolen," Cadman said,
"but neither group would confirm it. What was it the
FBI called their questions? Background, I think. No, I
don't mind talking to you about Voynich, because you
understand the importance of these things. The FBI
acted as if the manuscript were a stolen car—make,
model, color, dollar value—while all the fascists wanted
to know was how to read it."

"Read it?"

"Yes. The best minds have been working for years
on trying to decipher it, and they were under the impression there ought to be something like conversational
Voynichese available."

"I'm afraid that I probably don't know much more,"
Indy admitted. "Could you start with the beginning?
Who found it and where?"

"For some reason, Voynich kept the details of the find a secret," Cadman said. "He died three years ago. But a few months before his death, he confided to me that he discovered the manuscript in 1912 in a sort of treasure chest at the Villa Mondragone, which is an old Jesuit seminary near Rome. It had apparently been at the seminary for two and a half centuries before my old friend found it, and at first he didn't know what to make of it. Neither did the Jesuits who sold it to him.

"The manuscript is one hundred and two pages, on vellum, with a text apparently written in a secret script. Interspersed are about four hundred enigmatic drawings —astrological, botanical, biological. It is richly colored —blue, green, red, what have you. There are pictures of stars, and plants, and some interesting naked ladies in what look like bathtubs. The manuscript was merely a curiosity for a time, until in 1921 a fellow by the name of Newbold claimed that he had deciphered it and it was the work of Roger Bacon."

"The thirteenth-century alchemist and Franciscan monk," Indy said.

"Newbold, as you probably know, made some pretty wild claims. He said that Bacon had used microscopes and telescopes—hundreds of years before their documented invention—and had cracked many of the mysteries of modern science. Newbold said the message was embedded in a kind of Roman shorthand hidden in the text, but nobody else could produce the same results. It eventually ruined his career, and he died in 1926."

"The manuscript seems to have claimed its share of victims," Indy mused.

"It has," Cadman agreed. "Although I believe Newbold died more from a broken heart than from any Tut-like curse. It has ruined a good many careers—those who study it for too long seem to become deluded into seeing what they hope to find. Still, after Wilfrid Voynich died, the fear of calamity may have inspired his widow to place the manuscript on permanent loan at Yale—simply to get it out of the house."

Indy sipped his tea.

"What do you think of the manuscript?" he asked.

"I *do* think it is an alchemical text, although probably not the work of Roger Bacon. To an experienced eye, there are too many clues that the time period is wrong. One can only guess as to where it originated."

"Your smile tells me that you have a theory."

"Just a theory," Cadman said. "But there is some evidence that it is likely to be the same manuscript that appeared in Prague about 1608. Rudolph the Second bought it from a pair of English alchemists, John Dee and Edward Kelley. You know of them?"

Indy shook his head.

"Pity. They are among the more colorful characters of the period—charlatans, many said—although Dee was regarded as the most educated man in England and was court astrologer to Queen Elizabeth. Kelley claimed he found an undecipherable manuscript in a tomb in Wales, along with a vial of red powder he called the elixir of life, after which Kelley became adept at scrying —an old word for fortune-telling—with the aid of something called the Shew Stone."

"The Shew Stone?"

"Yes. It was a piece of New World crystal that Dee had acquired, and with it, Kelley claimed to be able to commune with angels and see the future. They recorded

a supposedly angelic language called Enochian, which
the Rosicrucians still use. Dee's son, John, later recalled
that his father and Kelley spent much of their time with
the stone attempting to decipher a mysterious book that
was written in hieroglyphics."

"I suppose this stone has been lost to the ages,"
Indy mused.

"Oh, no," Cadman said. "It's on display at the British Museum in London. Dee and Kelley are the ones
who actually planted the seed for attributing Voynich to
Roger Bacon. They held Bacon in high regard and, before selling the manuscript for six hundred gold ducats
to Rudolph at Prague, leaked rumors that it was written
by him and contained the secret of turning lead into
gold. Tradition has it that they even succeeded in this,
although it was no doubt some clever sleight of hand."

"It seems to me that if they could make their own
gold," Indy said, "there would be no need to sell the
manuscript—they could be as rich as they wanted without having to part with it."

"That, my friend, has given the lie to alchemy
throughout the ages," Cadman said. "It's something that
a six-year-old could recognize, but a power-mad king
could not."

"Whatever else you say about Dee and Kelley,"
Indy said, "you have to admire their salesmanship. They
could make a fortune selling life insurance today. What
became of this pair?"

"After being arrested on charges of sorcery and her-
esy, Kelley was imprisoned by Rudolph at Prague—but
he was allowed to have his mysterious books, because
the king still wanted him to make gold. Kelley attempted

to escape from the prison, but fell from a rooftop and died.

"Dee fared somewhat better. He returned to England, continued to practice sorcery and alchemy, but could not make the old magic work without his friend. He died in disrepute."

"What happened to the manuscript?"

"Rudolph died in 1612, and at the time it was apparently in the possession of Jacobus de Tepenecz, director of the king's alchemical laboratory. Sometime between 1622 and 1656, the manuscript was willed to Joannus Marcus Marci, Rudolph's court physician. Marci sent it to his old teacher, Athanius Kircher, at Rome—one of the great alchemists of the seventeenth century. When Kircher became a Jesuit in 1660, he gave away all his worldly goods, and the manuscript sat on the shelf in the seminary near Rome until it was found by Voynich."

"So, we have from about 1608 to 1933 accounted for. Are we to assume that it was written in the sixteenth or seventeenth century?"

Cadman smiled.

"Oh, the manuscript itself is probably four or five hundred years old, but it is probably a copy of something that is much more ancient."

"How ancient?"

"From the first or second century at least, perhaps even before the birth of Christ," he said. "Alchemical lore seems to have been handed down in a number of forms since nearly the beginning of recorded history. In the West, for example, there is a fable that Alexander the Great discovered the philosopher's stone in a cave. Arab sources credit their own heroes with this. And the Chinese—well, they have their own wealth of alchemical tradition. Would you care for some more tea?"

Cadman went to the hot plate, returned with the kettle, and poured more steaming water in both of their cups. Indy yawned and looked at his watch. It was a quarter to three.

"We could continue this tomorrow," Cadman suggested.

"No," Indy said. "Please, if you're up to it—"

"Of course I'm up to it. The night is young. Frankly, I don't have many people to talk to these days—I guess I frighten most of them away. Most people are such dolts, don't you agree? One finds so few good listeners."

"I'm curious—what did you tell the FBI and the others?"

"Nothing, practically," Cadman said. "They asked questions as if they were asking the price of a piece of round steak. The fools didn't know they weren't asking the *right* question—that is, what I know. And I know a great deal about the past, which comes from having spent a lifetime with books that haven't been read in generations."

The glass in the front door rattled. Indy, who was sitting with his back to the door, glanced over his shoulder and thought he saw a shadow darting away.

"Just the wind," Cadman said.

"I'm sure," Indy said. "But if you don't mind— could we move away from the light? I'm afraid that all of this cloak-and-dagger business lately has made me a bit edgy."

They moved their chairs and their tea away from the desk and its bare bulb hanging overhead, to behind a shelf of books that concealed them from prying eyes.

Indy judged the row of books to be thick enough to stop any caliber of slug short of a howitzer.

"Can you think of any reason," he asked, "why someone would want to steal the manuscript?"

"Why anyone would steal the manuscript baffles me," Cadman said. "There are a number of copies of the work available, and its worth as a collectible—well, that amounts to a few thousand dollars, at most. Hardly justifies having the FBI breathing down your neck."

"What could possessing the manuscript itself provide that a copy would not?" Indy asked.

"Perhaps there's something hidden inside the vellum, or some other key that is not apparent to photographic reproduction," Cadman said. "A chemical reaction of some sort couldn't be ruled out—you know, the old disappearing-and-reappearing-ink trick. They certainly had the capacity five hundred years ago, and an alchemist would be the logical candidate for *that*. Or, it could be optical—hold it up to the light a certain way, or in a certain color of light. It could be almost anything, or nothing. There is always the possibility that Voynich is a five-hundred-year-old hoax."

Indy nodded.

"It would be my guess," Cadman continued, "that even if someone did manage to decipher the thing, the information it contained probably is useless to anyone who is not intimately familiar with alchemical lore. The alchemists were fond of couching their knowledge in riddles, to protect it from the eyes of the impure—'That Which Is Above Is Below' is a rather well-known example. Then there's the question of the *prima materia,* the first matter that is used to make the stone. Nobody has ever been able to identify what exactly that was, although the riddles hinted that it was something that, once discovered, would be painfully obvious—at one's feet, as it were."

"Then you believe there's a good chance that Voynich contains the secret to making the philosopher's stone?"

"No decent alchemical text would be without it," Cadman said. "The fabled philosopher's stone, with the ability to transmute lead into gold and grant immortality. It's quite a pretty dream, isn't it?"

"It would be," Indy said, "if it were true."

"Actually," Cadman said, "we probably should give alchemy more credit than modern science is willing to admit. Despite the hokum, the secrets encoded in riddles and the outlandish claims, it got the ball rolling for science to take over. All those beakers and retorts and vials in the modern lab—all came from alchemy." He raised his cup of tea.

"A toast then, to alchemy," he said. .

"And to help from strangers," Indy said, and joined the toast.

"Tell me," Cadman said. "Did you really come here seeking a room? Or was it merely a clever ruse?"

"I came for a room," Indy said, "but I was seeking . . . I don't know. Direction, perhaps."

"Ah, a meaningful coincidence," Cadman said. "Synchronicity, if you believe Jung. There are no accidents, my friend."

"Perhaps," Indy said. "Although providence seems an easier word for it. Whatever it is, I'm not going to question it—where else would one find an expert on a dead art in the middle of the night?"

"Not quite dead," Cadman said. "Alchemy has undergone a sort of modest revival since Lord Rutherford succeeded in transmuting nitrogen into oxygen using high-energy radioactivity—an act that Cartesian science said was impossible. Part of the reason I am conversant about this is because I have some very good clients who buy everything on the subject they can get their hands on."

"Really?" Indy asked.

"There is one fellow in London who is most probably the world's leading authority on the actual *practice* of alchemy. His name is Alistair Dunstin and he has a position of some sort at the British Museum. I'm regularly shipping things to him. There's even an absurd rumor that he's actually managed to turn a small amount of lead into gold."

"He could be worth talking to," Indy said.

"The Italians seemed to think so," Cadman said. "They asked me about him—what kinds of things I shipped to him and so forth. Of course, I didn't tell them anything."

"Of course," Indy said.

Cadman yawned, then stood and stretched.

"I'm afraid we have talked the night away."

Indy stood as well. He extended his hand.

"Thank you," he said. "You've been more of a help than you'll ever know. I hope someday to return the favor."

"There is one small thing," Cadman said. "If you wouldn't mind."

"What would that be?"

"Tell me your name," Cadman said.

3

LORDS OF THE SKY

On the narrow bed in the rented room, Indy lay thinking and waiting for daylight. Tired as he was, he couldn't sleep—he kept dwelling on the men in the gray uniforms and their guns, and Sarducci with his scarred bald head and the gleaming gold fang where his right front incisor had been. What was the connection, he wondered, between the men in the flying boat and the Voynich Manuscript? Indy had a bad feeling that he was being sucked into something that a cooler or wiser head would leave alone. But his curiosity was getting the better of him, and he was anxious to make up for lost time. When dawn finally broke he was shaved, dressed, and ready.

When he opened the door to the hall he heard the thud of footsteps retreating down the stairs, as if he had surprised someone. He hurried to the bottom of the stairs, and glanced in both directions, but the sidewalk was empty.

He slipped the key to the room beneath the door of Cadman's shop. The rising sun had restored the bearings he had lost the night before—if he went one block south and then continued east, he reckoned, he was bound to find Penn Station, which sprawled over the railway tracks from 31st to 33rd streets. He planned to retrieve his bags, change into fresh clothes, and then begin his search for the fascists with the big airplane. No need to contact the FBI or army intelligence until he knew more about what he was dealing with. . . .

With its massive Doric columns, Penn Station looked like an enormous Roman temple dropped into the heart of Manhattan, and the stairway leading to the main entrance was constructed from the same kind of cream-colored Italian stone that built the Colosseum. Indy hurried down the stairway and past the long arcade with its shops and vendors to the main waiting room, which was modeled after a Roman bath. The tracks were beneath the floor, and Indy could feel the throb of locomotives as they pulled in and out of the station. He slipped through the bustling crowd to the row of lockers and retrieved his suitcase and leather satchel.

Indy had emerged from the men's room, after changing into his khaki work clothes, when a newsboy hawking the morning edition of the *New York Journal* walked by. "Balbo Air Armada Leaves in Triumph," the boy called, reciting the forty-eight-point banner headline and its kicker: "Bound for Europe." He held a copy of the newspaper high over his head, and a four-column photograph above the fold showed a flock of massive twin-hulled seaplanes.

"Paper, mister?" the newsboy asked.

Indy paid for a copy.

"When did all of this happen?" Indy asked the newsboy. "How long have the Italian airplanes been in America?"

"Gee, mister, have you been in a cave for the last month?"

"Sort of," Indy said. "But it was an underground temple, not a cave, and I spent most of the time in the jungle getting there and back."

"You're goofy," the newsboy said, and hurried away.

Indy dropped his bags, fished his glasses from the breast pocket of his leather jacket, and stood immobile in the middle of the bustling crowd while he read.

Then he gathered his things and hurried to a bank of pay phones along the wall. He found a vacant spot and dropped a nickel into the box while searching his pockets for the business card Manly had given him.

"Yes, operator. Just a moment." He finally found the card where he had placed it for safekeeping, tucked into his wallet. "Thanks, I'll wait. . . . Major? This is Jones. How fast can you get me to the other side of the Atlantic?"

The airship U.S.S. *Macon* was a gleaming silver torpedo the length of two and one half football fields. On her sides were the familiar star-within-a-circle emblems of naval airpower, and the trailing edges of her tail fins were painted red, white, and blue. The American flag fluttered in the breeze beneath a gunport that bristled from her tail. The taxi that wheeled up beneath her belly at the U.S. Naval Air Station at Lakehurst, New Jersey, seemed like a toy in comparison.

The *Macon* had been towed out of her enormous, cocoonlike hangar and was slowly beginning to lift skyward for her maiden flight across the Atlantic. The navy would not permit her schedule to be delayed for the arrival of a last-minute civilian passenger, although it would grudgingly allow passage—if the tag-along could arrive on time.

When Indy had dashed out of Penn Station, he had hopped into a big Plymouth, the most powerful-looking automobile he could find among the row of taxis lined up at the curb. He had thrust a handful of money into the cabbie's hand—all of the cash that he had left—and ordered him to *drive*. The cabbie had been up to the challenge. From the moment the cab rocketed into morning traffic to the time it arrived at Lakehurst, less than an hour and fifteen minutes had passed. Even before the cab's wheels had ground to a stop on smoking black drums, Indy and his suitcase were out the door.

"What, no tip?" the cabbie snarled after him.

"Always signal before turning," Indy shouted back.

An army staff car was parked beneath the dirigible, and a fresh-faced lieutenant bounded out of the car to meet Indy. In his hand was a thick brown envelope.

"Dr. Jones," he said. "The major instructed me to give you this."

"Thanks." Indy tucked the envelope inside his jacket.

Teams of sailors holding fast to her mooring lines did a curious waltz across the field as the *Macon* drifted slightly on the wind. Then the dirigible's eight German-made Maybach engines began to sputter to life, and

puffs of dark smoke poured from the outboard exhausts.
The dirigible was not yet a hundred feet above, and the
wash from the massive props threatened to whisk Indy's
hat away. He grabbed his fedora with one hand.

"I'm sorry you didn't make it in time," the lieutenant said. Indy looked skyward. The aircraft hid the sun,
covering the field in an unnatural twilight; a fine mist
had been coming down all morning, but beneath the
Macon it was as dry as the proverbial powder house. She
was under power, and began to rise. On command, the
sailors were releasing the mooring lines, beginning with
the lines at her tail. The throb of the *Macon*'s engines
increased in pitch as the outrigger propellers, which
could swivel through ninety degrees, tilted upward for a
vertical takeoff.

"She's not gone yet," Indy said.

He hesitated a moment. A trio of husky sailors
struggled with the mooring line dangling from the dirigible's nose, waiting for the command to release.

"I know I'm going to hate this part," Indy said.

Clutching his suitcase, Indy sprinted across the
field while the lieutenant watched slack-jawed. The
megaphoned command was given to release the bow-
line, and the three sailors at the nose gave up their tug-
of-war with the giant. The line slipped across the grass
and then was free of the earth, the knotted end dangling
a few feet above the ground.

Indy ran harder.

He wedged his hat firmly on his head and grasped
the line with his right hand.

It seemed to have a life of its own.

Indy was jerked off of his feet. The toes of his shoes
dug lines in the turf while his right arm felt as if it were

being wrenched from its socket. Then his feet were swinging in the air. He flung away his suitcase and took hold of the line with his left hand as well.

The suitcase popped open when it hit the ground. His clothes, driven by the prop wash, danced across the field. The ground receded beneath Indy and his heart jumped into his throat when he realized that he was too high now to let go. The line was wet with mist and he slipped downward a few inches before regaining his hold. The memory of a grainy newspaper photo of two young seamen falling to their deaths from a mooring line of a dirigible at San Diego gave him inspired strength. He pulled himself higher, hand over hand, until he could wrap his ankles around the line. His left shoe fell off, and Indy had to force himself not to watch as it plunged earthward.

Astonished faces peered at him through the forward windows of the control car. There was momentary confusion as flight engineer and navigator argued about whether to set the airship down.

"No," said Commander Alger Dresel, and urged a steady course. "The wind is too stiff for this kind of terrain. We're likely to drag him through trees or flatten him against the side of a building. The fool stands a better chance on his own."

The pilot nodded.

"Get some men forward to haul him in," Dresel said.

Indy shinnied up the line.

Two hundred feet separated him from the hull of the *Macon*. His arms ached, but he had no choice but to continue. The sailors who watched from the winch platform at the nose couldn't help, because the mooring lines dangled from the hull, a dozen yards out of reach.

Indy paused at the halfway point, letting his feet take his weight while he gave his arms and shoulders a brief rest. Then he forced himself on. Finally he was level with the bottom of the hull, but because of the rounded shape of the *Macon*, he was still hanging far out on the starboard side. It was raining in earnest now, and he shook his head to fling the water from his eyes. He searched the hull above him for some type of porthole or hatch, but the silver skin of the *Macon* appeared to be unbroken.

He continued to climb.

The gap between him and the hull grew narrower, to just a few yards. Then the airship rolled slightly to port, under the delicate touch of the elevator pilot's hand on the trim wheels, and Indy found himself resting against its side.

With one hand he groped at the varnished fabric skin, searching for a handhold, but his fingernails skittered across the smooth wet surface. In desperation he withdrew his pocketknife, opened it with his teeth, and drove the blade as hard as he could into the side of the ship. It pierced the fabric. He flinched involuntarily, halfway expected an explosion or the rush of gas, but nothing happened. He put his weight on the knife and cut a three-foot slit.

"There he is!" he heard someone shout from inside.

A hand reached through the slit, grasped the front of his leather jacket, and hauled him inside. Indy released his grip on the rope. The edges of the fabric were like sandpaper and scraped his left cheek as he passed through.

He found himself inside the aluminum-girdered web of the starboard lateral gangway, which ran the length of the ship. Overhead were the massive helium cells.

A group of men stood over him.

"That was some stunt you pulled," said the broad-shouldered sailor who had pulled him in. "I've never seen anybody make it before. Mister, you must have wanted to ride a zep really badly."

Indy had wanted to say there was a first time for everything, but couldn't manage to get the words out. He was shivering and couldn't feel his hands. He clumsily touched his face with the back of his hand and examined the drops of blood that had oozed from the scratches on his cheek. Then he turned both of his hands over. His palms were raw and bleeding.

"O'Toole, quit socializing," the crew chief barked. "And quit comparing my beautiful dirigible to a stinking, flaming, hydrogen-filled zeppelin."

"Sorry, chief."

"Get him down to quarters and get him cleaned up," ordered the crew chief. "The commander would like to see him. And you two, start getting that hole patched up. Imagine cutting the skin of my beautiful new airship just to let in a *civilian.*"

O'Toole helped Indy to his feet and led him down the gangway to the crew quarters, above the hangar deck. He showed him a bunk and poured a strong cup of hot coffee while Indy pulled off his wet clothes. He provided towels and a clean pair of dungarees, then returned with a medical kit.

"Hurt?" O'Toole asked as he treated Indy's palms with iodine.

"I can't feel them," Indy said.

"You will." O'Toole wrapped Indy's hands in cloth bandages, then shook some tablets from a medicine bottle. "Here, take some aspirin."

The aspirin were chalky and caught in Indy's throat and he had to swallow two mouthfuls of coffee to get them down. The coffee began to stoke a fire in his belly.

"Much obliged."

"Don't mention it," O'Toole said. "I know what it's like to be hanging for your life on the side of a zep—I mean, an airship. I was on board the *Akron* a couple of months ago when she broke her back on the water. She sank in three minutes."

"I read about it," Indy said.

"It was night, during a thunderstorm, and the sea was cold," O'Toole said. "There were seventy-six men onboard. Only three of us made it."

"What happened?" Indy asked. "I mean, why did you go down?"

"Our elevator cables parted. Then something happened to the altimeter—it said we were at eight hundred feet when our tail hit the water. The navy brass concluded that a freak low-pressure front scrambled the instruments, but I'm not so sure, because eight hundred feet seems like a heck of a mistake to me."

Indy nodded.

He glanced idly around the cabin. On O'Toole's bunk there was a catcher's mitt, and beneath the mattress the white pine handle of a baseball bat protruded.

"You a baseball fan?" Indy asked.

"Am I!" O'Toole said, and withdrew the bat. It was a genuine Louisville Slugger. "I play every chance I get. There's enough room on the hangar deck, but the balls go into the drink every once in a while. This is my baby, Thunder Stick, and she's never let me down."

There was a knock on the cabin door.

O'Toole kissed the bat and replaced it beneath the mattress.

Commander Dresel entered. O'Toole stood at attention and saluted. Dresel returned the salute.

"Back to your duties, seaman."

"Aye, sir," O'Toole said. He gave Indy a wink before leaving the cabin.

"Dr. Jones," Dresel said, sitting down on the bunk across from him. "If you pull any more shenanigans like you did this morning, I will be forced to set you down— even if it is adrift in a rubber raft in the middle of the Atlantic. There is no place for such foolish grandstanding on my ship."

"Commander," Indy said, "I apologize for my unorthodox entry, but it was imperative that I be onboard. I am operating under the authority of army intelligence, and Major Manly assured me of your cooperation."

"The army," Dresel said sourly.

"Yes, sir."

"Where's the fire, Jones? Surely you could have booked other passage across the Atlantic. Passenger ships, I understand, are quite good at keeping regular schedules."

"There isn't a ship afloat that could get me across in forty-eight hours," Indy said. "The fire, as you say, is something of an international nature—it's been smoldering in Europe for quite some time now."

Dresel grunted.

"While you're onboard my ship," the commander

said, "you will be under my command. At no point are
you to endanger the ship or its crew with any unauthorized activity. You may mess with the crew, and sleep in
this cabin, but you *will* behave yourself. Is that understood?"

"Quite," Indy said.

"Are you armed?"

"I beg your pardon?"

"You heard me. Do you have a sidearm?"

"Well, yes, sir," Indy said. A new Webley revolver
was in his leather satchel.

"Hand it over," Dresel said. "I will keep it in the
locked safe in my cabin until you disembark, at which
time you will get it back."

Indy took the revolver out of the satchel, opened
the cylinder, and removed the shells. He decided it was
best not to mention the bullwhip. He handed the gun
and the ammunition to Dresel.

"The control car and the aircraft hangar are off-
limits. Otherwise, you may have the run of the ship,"
Dresel said. "Manly told me you are bound for London.
That is not a scheduled stop for us, but we are passing
close by. The final leg of your journey will be completed
in a Sparrowhawk, which will set you on the ground and
then return to the ship."

"That is as close to Rome as you can get me?" Indy
asked.

"The last thousand miles shouldn't be a problem,"
Dresel said, "for someone of your resourcefulness."

"Tell me, Commander," Indy said. "The *Akron*—
she was the sister ship to the *Macon*?"

"Affirmative. The *Akron* was built first and had

been flying for about a year and a half," Dresel said. "The designs are the same, but the *Macon* uses the new gelatin-latex fabric for her gas cells. They're helium, you know—the U.S. has a corner on the market—and it can't explode like hydrogen does, which the Germans have to use for their ships. Are you worried about the airworthiness of the *Macon*?"

"No, sir. I was just curious."

"The *Macon* is the navy's newest and finest dirigible, and incidentally is also the largest aircraft of any type in the world," Dresel said. "We have a top speed of eighty-five miles an hour, and a range of ten thousand miles. In the hangar below us are a squadron of Curtiss Sparrowhawk fighter planes, which are specially equipped to be deployed and picked up in flight. It works on a trapeze mechanism, and there's even a perch for planes that are waiting their turn. We are the eyes in the sky for the navy, and with our improved design, we are quite literally unsinkable."

"Unsinkable?"

"In a word, yes."

"That's what they said about the *Titanic*."

Dresel smiled.

"There are no icebergs up here," he said.

With another cup of strong coffee from the mess, Indy returned to the cabin and took from his satchel the envelope that Manly had sent. His hands were beginning to hurt now, and he had trouble opening the sealed flap. The documents inside were stamped in red: SECRET— EYES ONLY. On top of the stack of papers was a glossy black-and-white photograph of Sarducci and Benito Mussolini. Il Duce's hand rested stiffly on Sarducci's shoulder. There was a handwritten note from Manly paper-clipped to the photograph.

Jones, the note read.

Here is your man. He is a brilliant but insane Renaissance scholar who is now working for OVRA, Mussolini's secret police. Sarducci is an ultra-fascist whose motto is 'violence is the best expression of creativity.' Good luck—and do be careful.

Indy flipped through the rest of the material. He stopped at a dossier on Sarducci.

SARDUCCI, LEONARDO. Italian minister of the archaic for Benito Mussolini. Born to a peasant family October 31, 1892, at Fascati, Italy. Attended public school and studied at the Sorbonne, but failed his oral examinations in Renaissance literature by refusing to submit to the authority of his French professors. Later received a doctorate from the University of Rome. Married Mona Grimaldi in 1913. Taught university courses in Rome until the beginning of World War I, when he joined the Italian army as a captain. Suffered a near-fatal head wound in the trenches. Returned to Rome after his discharge to discover that his wife, Mona, had died of sepsis during childbirth. This trauma, complicated by mental problems resulting from the head wound, resulted in a personality collapse. He began a public denunciation of science and medicine, which culmi-

nated in a brutal attack upon the physician who was attendant during his wife's labor; after drugging the doctor, he removed his hands with a meat cleaver, claiming that since he had not learned to wash them between patients, he apparently did not need them. Sarducci was committed to a prison for the criminally insane from 1918 to 1921, during which he spent his time writing a treatise on the wisdom of the archaic and denouncing modern intellectualism and what he called "the fallacy of empiricism." The book was a best-seller among those in the anti-intellectual fascist movement, and drew the praise of no less than Mussolini himself, who described Sarducci as a sort of folk hero for his act of vengeance upon the doctor blamed for his wife's death. Sarducci was released from prison following Mussolini's rise to power in 1922, and became a cult figure of extraordinary power within the fascist movement. He was named minister of the archaic in 1927 and became the spiritual leader of the Fascisti's war against socialists, communists, Catholics, liberals, and intellectuals.

Indy whistled.

There was another, briefer file describing Italo Balbo, the mastermind of the Italian air armada that had crossed the Atlantic to visit Chicago and New York. Balbo had been named Mussolini's air minister in 1929. He had developed the Italian air force in 1923 and organized mass demonstration flights to Brazil in 1930 and, recently, the United States. Balbo called his elite cadre of airmen the *atlantici,* and they were regarded as the best-trained of any European power. Balbo's armada of twenty-four SIAI-Marchetti SM.55A aircraft (and Balbo's personal aircraft, an SM.55X experimental, with the designation I-BALB) had completed a transatlantic tour that included Chicago and New York. The armada had left the Coney Island seaplane base on its return to Italy at 5:25 that morning.

Balbo had been showered by gifts and honors on each leg of the flight. He was given a ticker-tape parade down Broadway and had addressed a crowd of sixty thousand at Madison Square Garden. "Italians of New York," he had proclaimed, "Mussolini has ended the period of humiliations, and to be Italian is now a sign of honor. Respect the tricolor and the star-spangled banner. Our two nations, which have never been divided in the past, have never been closer, nor will the future ever divide us." Balbo had even lunched with President Franklin Roosevelt at the White House. His popularity at home and abroad had aroused Mussolini's jealousy— he even wanted Balbo to renounce the honor of having a major street in Chicago named after him—and there were rumors that Il Duce would soon exile him by naming him governor of Libya or one of the other Italian holdings in North Africa.

A photograph showed I-BALB with the following information taped beneath: *SM.55X. Long-range flying boat. Engines: two 12-cylinder, 800-horsepower, liquid-cooled. Wingspan: 78 ft. 9 in. Length: 54 ft. 1 in. Weight: 22,000 lb. Crew: four. Range: 2,400 miles.* The numbers seemed to run together until he came to the last entry: *Cruising Speed: 149 mph.*

Indy uttered a schoolboy's curse.

He searched through the papers until he found a map that showed the armada's route. Instead of flying directly from New York to Rome, which was beyond the SM.55's range, they would skirt the North American coast and refuel in Nova Scotia. From there would begin a dangerous 1,700-mile journey to Ponta Delgada, an island refueling station in the North Atlantic, and then on to Lisbon, a thousand miles away. The final leg of the journey was a 1,400-mile tour of the Mediterranean to Rome.

"They're faster than we are," he said to himself. "But they have to stop to refuel twice, and we're going straight across."

Indy stretched out on the bunk to think. The gentle hum of the motors was soothing, and there was no sensation of speed or movement. The bunk beneath him felt as steady, he thought, as his bed in the little rented house at 1226 Chestnut back at Princeton. . . .

Something roused Indy from uneasy dreams. A bump, perhaps, or a kind of muffled jar. He bolted upright, held up his hands in the darkness, and touched his face to reassure himself that they were still attached. He stumbled groggily to the cabin window. It was night, and the moon shimmered on the sea far below. The phosphorescent wake of a ship—he couldn't tell what kind, but it appeared to be a large one—cut a wavering V on the surface of the water. To the east was a squall line, and thunderbolts lighted the interiors of the dark clouds with a pink neon glow.

"You all right, Professor?" O'Toole asked, popping in the cabin door.

"I thought I felt something," Indy said. "A bump."

"Probably just rough air," O'Toole said. "We're heading into a storm."

Indy nodded.

"Hungry?" O'Toole asked. "You slept through dinner."

"Starved," Indy replied. He gathered the intelligence files, placed them back into the satchel, and slung the leather bag over his shoulder. Then he followed O'Toole to the mess.

"Where are we?" Indy asked over a plate of ham and beans.

"Middle of the Atlantic," O'Toole said. "Not quite halfway there. The weather's going to be rough, and it will add some time to the crossing."

"Tell me," Indy said between bites. "Is there any way on or off of the *Macon* at this point? I mean, are we within range of land for one of the Sparrowhawks?"

"Thinking of jumping ship?" O'Toole asked.

"No," Indy said. "I was considering the possibility of sabotage. It seems like the *Macon* is a rather large target and wouldn't be hard to find."

"Well, we're not close enough to landfall for the Sparrowhawks to make it," O'Toole said. "Say there was a saboteur onboard and he wanted to use one of the Sparrowhawks to make his escape—he would have to be a lot closer to land than we are now. Otherwise, it would be suicide."

"What about other planes?" Indy asked. "Not one of the Sparrowhawks, but one from the outside. Could it rendezvous with us?"

"Unlikely," O'Toole said. "It would take an expert pilot just to be able to dock with the trapeze mechanism. Besides, we're still too far from land. There's no small aircraft in the world that would have the kind of range needed."

"One of Balbo's flying boats couldn't do it, then."

"Not at all. It takes a small plane, a fighter aircraft."

"A scout, perhaps."

"Well, yes."

"Some ships carry scouts, don't they?"

"A lot of them do."

Indy left the table and went to the windows along the galley wall. The *Macon* was passing through a cloud bank, but an occasional break in the clouds revealed that the wake from the ship was still visible.

"Can you make out what kind of ship that is?" he asked.

O'Toole took a pair of binoculars from the sill and held them to his eyes. He studied the ship for a few seconds, then handed the lenses to Indy.

"It's a medium-sized warship," he said. "Can't tell exactly what." He went to a telephone at the bulkhead.

"Chief?" he asked. "Have you been keeping tabs on the sea traffic? Do you know what warship that is below us?" O'Toole placed his hand over the mouthpiece. "He's checking with bridge. . . . Yeah, I'm here. An Italian submarine hunter? Right. Thanks, chief."

"Submarine hunters carry scouts," Indy said. "The hangar's directly below the galley and the crew quarters. Is there a hatch or something?"

"No, it's just a big aircraft-shaped hole."

"Is the hangar guarded?"

"We've never felt the need," O'Toole said. "The hangar deck would be secured and deserted in weather like this, because there's too much of a chance of somebody falling overboard. Professor, are you thinking that bump could mean something?"

"I don't know. Wouldn't anybody else feel it?"

"Might not," O'Toole said. "When the tail of the *Akron* hit the water, we hardly felt it at all. The ship has a way of absorbing vibration, unless you're right on top of it."

"You need to search the hangar deck," Indy said.

"Commander won't go for it, not in weather like this," O'Toole said. "He'd think the idea was preposterous. I think it's kind of goofy myself."

Indy grunted.

"You'd be surprised at some of the things that happen to me," he said. "I can't ask you to disobey orders, but *I'm* going to have a look."

"Now, Professor. The skipper said that was off-limits."

"I've got a bad feeling," Indy said. "Contact the bridge and tell them I need help on the hangar deck."

"Not me," O'Toole said. "They'd skin me alive if they knew I let you go there."

Indy left the mess. He hurried down the flight of stairs to the hangar deck. It was cold and deserted. The five Sparrowhawk biplanes were tied down in a semicircle, facing the aircraft bay. Clouds and mist billowed up from below. The trapeze hook was secured to the overhead rail system that lifted the planes in and out of the airship, and there appeared to be no way that an aircraft could dock unannounced with the *Macon*.

Indy walked cautiously around the perimeter of the aircraft bay, not quite knowing what he was looking for, but he had the distinct feeling that somebody was watching *him*. He knelt at the edge of the hatch and peered out, but could see nothing in the darkness.

Suddenly a bolt of lightning streaked across the sky, illuminating the belly of the *Macon* like a giant flashbulb. The silhouette of a single-wing airplane hanging from the aircraft perch just aft of the hangar was burned into Indy's retinas.

Spots danced before his eyes.

Indy scooted backward, feeling his way with his hands along the hangar floor. He couldn't see a thing. He shook his head, rubbed his eyes with the backs of his hands, and still could make out nothing but blurs around him.

Footsteps sounded behind him.

"O'Toole?" Indy called hopefully.

The footsteps drew closer.

"Who's there?" he demanded.

"*Eccomi, Dottore Jones!*" an Italian voice said. "Here I am! My name is Mario Volatore. You killed my brother Marco. Now it is your turn to die."

A boot caught Indy beneath the chin, sending him sprawling on his back. He struggled to his feet, but a fist to the temple sent him down again.

"It was ingenious how we modified our aircraft to lock onto your American dirigible, no?" Mario asked. "Who would have suspected? Who would notice it in a storm such as this? What a tragedy! They will say it was a design flaw, such as the one that took her doomed sister *Akron*."

Indy was ready for the next kick. His sight was returning, and he saw the blur of Mario's foot as it came toward his face. He caught the boot in both hands and twisted viciously. Mario landed heavily on the deck.

"Bravo!" Mario called. "You want to make a fight of it!"

Mario was bigger and stronger than Marco had been. A thick black mustache sprouted from his upper lip, and he was dressed all in black. From the deck he picked up a spanner some careless mechanic had left behind.

Indy hit him twice in the face, but Mario's head barely moved.

"Ah, you're wearing gloves," Mario said. "How sporting!"

The spanner swung in a wide arc and Indy ducked beneath it. He could feel the wind from it stir the hair on the top of his head. Quickly he tore off the bandages that covered both hands and came up swinging.

He gave Mario two lefts followed by a right, and they all carried with them the satisfying smack of knuckles against bare skin. Mario staggered back, dropping the wrench.

"Did Sarducci radio ahead and have you intercept us?" Indy asked.

"Of course," Mario said, shaking his head. "He was quite displeased to learn that you were not dead. He was afraid that he had told you far too much during your brief encounter."

Mario advanced and feinted with his left, then dropped to the floor and used his powerful legs to sweep Indy's feet from beneath him. He was on top of Indy in an instant, pinning him to the hangar deck.

He drew an automatic pistol and held it to Indy's head.

"I would shoot you, but the noise would alert the

others," Mario said. "So I will have to be content with pushing you overboard. From this height, you will free-fall for three minutes and forty-five seconds before plunging into the sea. But don't worry—you won't drown. The impact of hitting the water from this height will certainly kill you."

Mario eased to his knees and pushed the gun barrel into the soft space beneath Indy's chin, urging him toward the hatch.

"I would stay and fight, but alas—there is no time."

Mario backhanded Indy with the gun barrel, and Indy fell into the hatch. His right hand caught the lip of the deck, and he dangled from one arm over the sea. The wind and rain lashed at him.

Mario looked at his wristwatch.

"In five minutes, all of this will be gone. *Come si chiama*—how is it called?—*la bomba?*" Mario ground the sole of his boot against Indy's knuckles.

"What will you think of during your four minutes on the way down?" he asked. "So brief, and yet such an eternity! Will you see the face of the woman you last made love to, or will you call out for your mother and father?"

Indy looked over Mario's shoulder.

"O'Toole!" he shouted.

"There's no one behind me. Do you think I'm a—" Mario began. The word *fool* came out as an unintelligible grunt as O'Toole hit him as hard as he could with his Louisville Slugger. Mario's head sounded as hollow as a watermelon. The gun flew out of his hand as he fell facedown on the hangar floor. He didn't move.

"Home run," O'Toole said. He kicked the gun out

of Mario's reach. Then he knelt and firmly pulled Indy
up into the hangar.

"Second time I've had to haul you in, Professor,"
O'Toole said. "What exactly do you teach, circus acrobat-
ics?"

"There's a bomb," Indy gasped. "We've got less
than five minutes. Call Dresel and get a search going,
now!"

Indy turned Mario over and slapped his face until
he came around.

"Where is it?" he demanded.

"A very good location," Mario said.

"Tell me!"

"The skipper is on his way," O'Toole called from
the bulkhead telephone. Indy made a fist, but the look in
Mario's eyes told him it would do no good.

Indy picked up the gun and tossed it to O'Toole.

"Watch him," he said. Indy began searching in and
around the planes.

"He could have gotten to anywhere on the ship,"
O'Toole said.

"We have to look anyway," Indy said.

All of the hangar lights came on as Commander
Dresel and his staff walked in.

"Jones!" Dresel called. "What is the meaning of
this?"

"There's a bomb onboard," Indy said.

"We caught this monkey on his way out," O'Toole
said, jerking the gun barrel toward Mario. "But he won't
tell us anything."

"How the devil did he get onboard?" Dresel asked.

"No time to explain, Commander," Indy said. He
looked at his watch. "We've got about three minutes."

Dresel signaled general quarters. Klaxons sounded and the intercoms crackled with orders as the search began. Mario chuckled at the confusion.

"You don't have time to find it," he said.

"Then you'll die with us," Indy said.

"Gladly."

Lightning crackled across the sky below them, followed by a shock wave of thunder. Dresel stood silently as he waited, his hands locked behind his back. O'Toole leaned on his bat and kept the gun trained on Mario while glancing anxiously toward Indy.

"Two minutes," Indy said.

Dresel regarded Mario with a look of disgust.

"I've never given this order before," he said. "But the lives of seventy-eight men are at stake here. Seaman O'Toole, you may beat it out of him."

"Aye aye, sir."

O'Toole shouldered the bat and advanced on Mario while two seamen held him. Mario twisted and broke free of their grasp, then leaped into the chasm.

He caught the trapeze mechanism with both hands and hung for a moment, regarding Indy and the others. A smile came to his face as he released his grip.

"*Spazio!*" he called, then dropped out of sight.

"Just terrific," Indy said. "Skipper, if you were going to plant a bomb to finish the *Macon* and make it look like an accident, where would you put it?"

Dresel thought.

"I'd put it in the channel containing the control lines to the tail, to disable the rudder and elevators. We'd crash like a rock into the sea."

"Where's the closest place to do that?"

"Not far," Dresel said. He and O'Toole were already running.

When Indy caught up to them, in the gangway behind the hangar deck, O'Toole was crawling through an inspection hatch with a flashlight.

"I found it," he said.

He passed out a bundle that contained five sticks of dynamite wired to a black box. O'Toole started to pull the wires apart, but Indy shouted for him not to.

"Pull the wrong ones and it'll go off," he explained.

"Get it overboard," Dresel suggested calmly.

A seaman snatched up the bundle and raced away.

Indy looked at his watch. There was no time left, but it seemed pointless to announce it. A few seconds either way would make the difference. There was nothing left to do but hold his breath.

An explosion sounded off the port side.

"Thank God," Dresel said.

"And Babe Ruth," O'Toole added.

Indy breathed again.

The monoplane hanging from the belly of the *Macon* was gone by the time they returned to the hangar deck. The pilot, abandoning Mario to his fate, had slipped the release and dropped silently into the storm.

"They'll never be able to recover the plane in seas like this," Dresel said. "Too bad, because I would have liked to have handed the pilot over to naval intelligence." He turned to Indy and shook his head.

"Jones, I appreciate your quick thinking here, but I'll be damned glad when you're off my ship. Trouble seems to be your middle name."

"Actually, no," Indy said.

"Professor," O'Toole said. "What was it that our monkey shouted before he fell into the drink?"

"The fascist war cry," Indy said. "*Spazio.* It's Italian for space, for territory—for elbow room."

"Well, he got it," O'Toole said. "It is a long way down."

4

SOROR MYSTICA

A Sparrowhawk fighter put Indy down on an airfield outside of London just as dawn was breaking. The crossing aboard the *Macon* had been uneventful following the attempted bombing, and Indy had spent the remaining time poring over the intelligence files and visiting the radio shack for updates about the progress of Balbo's armada. Luck, finally, had seemed to be on his side; bad weather had forced Balbo to lay over for three days at Ponta Delgada. Indy reached London while Balbo was still in the middle of the Atlantic.

Indy had the *Macon*'s radio operator send a coded message to Manly at army intelligence, informing him of the bombing attempt and asking him to contact Marcus Brody at the museum. Brody was to have the museum wire money to the Bank of England, enough to arrange passage to Rome and beyond. Indy asked that the funds be designated as working capital for an expedition to the

Isle of Wight, to have a ready explanation if anyone should inquire about his activities in England.

"You're lucky," the Sparrowhawk pilot told him as the fighter plane was being refueled. "A few months from now, we wouldn't be able to put you down. The navy has plans to remove the landing gear from all of the Sparrowhawks and replace them with long-range fuel tanks. I was sucking vapors to get you this far."

The grass airfield was twenty miles west of London and there was not so much as a single taxi available. The field operator—a World War I veteran who was also the mechanic and the man who pumped the aviation fuel— seemed wholly unconcerned about Indy's transport to the city. There was a rail station nearby, but that required money, and Indy was flat broke until he reached the Bank of England.

Indy set off down the road toward the east, hitchhiking. It was a cold morning and he thrust his hands in his coat pockets and turned his collar against the wind.

He had been walking for only a mile when a milk truck stopped.

The driver gave him a pint of milk for breakfast and, when he learned that Indy was an archaeologist, was anxious to display his knowledge of history. "Londinium," he said as they neared the city. "That's what the Romans called it in the first century. This was all wilderness, once," the driver said with a sweep of his hand. "The ends of the earth—can you imagine what it must have been like for those poor legionnaires, so far from their homes and families, fighting a pack of us blue-faced devils?"

"History repeats itself," Indy said. "Let a handful of

centuries pass, and then it's a British soldier who is fighting the Zulus in Africa."

"Or Belfast," the driver grunted. "You know, I laugh every time I see Mussolini in the newsreels. He is such a stiff-armed clown. But they'd like to resurrect the days of Imperial Rome, and that is not such a funny thought."

The driver's route went no farther than Chelsea, but he gave Indy a couple of bus tokens and wished him luck. Indy asked for his address so that he could repay him, but the driver simply waved good-bye.

Indy got off the double-decker bus on Tottenham Court Road in Bloomsbury, and although he was still three blocks away, he could see the imposing Greek facade of the British Museum rising like a sentinel beyond the trees.

He hurried through the sleepy residential district and was soon climbing the museum steps.

The interior was a labyrinth of wings and corridors that had been added over the years. Indy paused at the building directory in the entrance hall, but the listing of the various departments did him little good, since he had no idea where in the museum Alistair Dunstin might work.

"Pardon me," he said, addressing a middle-aged woman at the information booth. "Could you tell me where I can find Alistair Dunstin?"

"Dunstin," the woman repeated. She looked along her nose, through the bottom lenses in a pair of bifocals, and consulted a telephone list. "There's a Dunstin who is employed in the reading room. Shall I ring for you?"

"No, thanks. I prefer to announce myself."

"Straight inside," the woman said helpfully. "It's the only room in the entire building you can't miss."

Indy walked down the hallway to the cavernous library. In the center of the room, at a desk that looked as if it had already been there when Napoleon was defeated at Waterloo, Indy stopped.

"I'm looking for Alistair Dunstin," he said.

"Who isn't?" asked the librarian behind the desk.

"I beg your pardon?"

The young woman frowned.

"The sign on your desk," Indy said. "It says A. DUNSTIN. I'd like to see him."

"I'm *Alecia* Dunstin," the woman said, brushing a lock of red hair from her eyes. She had a lilting British accent that was mixed with something Indy couldn't identify; she had spent part of her youth in India, perhaps, or East Africa. "You're looking for my brother, Alistair. His office is upstairs, in British and Medieval Antiquities. But you won't find him there. He disappeared three days ago."

"Disappeared?"

"Lower your voice," she said. "This is a library."

"Sorry," Indy said. He felt like a schoolboy, standing in front of her desk and holding his hat in his hands. The great dome of the reading room of the British Museum stretched above them like the vault of heaven. Indy had a peculiar sensation, as if he were soliciting an angel for a moment of her time.

"Where has he gone?" he asked.

"I really don't think it's any of your business," she said. "There are other people in Antiquities who could help you, I'm sure."

"No, they can't."

Alecia Dunstin sighed. She had carefully avoided making eye contact, but now she found it impossible because the rude American in the scuffed leather jacket refused to leave. She skewered him with an icy stare from a pair of the bluest, palest eyes Indy had ever seen.

"Shall I call a bobby?" she asked.

Indy was momentarily disoriented. He had to look away from her in order to reply.

"Please listen," Indy said. "It's important that I find Alistair. He could be in danger because of his interest in something called the Voynich Manuscript. Perhaps you could give me an address or telephone number."

"I'm sorry, but that is not possible."

Indy looked back at her. Alecia Dunstin had begun to cry, but her voice was as controlled as if she were informing a patron that a certain book was unavailable.

"I'm sorry," Indy said. "I didn't mean to upset you."

"I don't need your sympathy," Alecia said, and wiped her eyes with the back of her hand. Her face was beginning to blotch. "Alistair is not on holiday. I told you, he has disappeared. Why do you keep badgering me so?"

"You mean he was kidnapped?"

"I don't know," she said. "He simply vanished. Everybody else thinks he ran away with that wretched manuscript. But I know Alistair too well to believe that. We're twins, you know."

"You don't think he stole it."

"Why am I telling you this?" she asked. This time it was she who raised her voice. "Who in bloody hell are you? You Americans are the rudest people I have ever dealt with. We haven't so much as been introduced, and already you're asking me questions about my private life. The amazing thing is, I'm answering them."

Patrons across the room turned from their books to see what the commotion was about. Alecia smiled and held a finger to her lips with a shrug.

"Perhaps you need someone to talk to," Indy suggested.

Her eyes softened.

"I'm Indiana Jones," he said.

"The archaeologist?" she asked. "I've heard of you."

"Really?" Indy asked.

"Actually, I have followed your career quite closely," she said. "I suppose I'm the only one here who actually reads those dreary old archaeological journals before I put them up. There is something about your panache which I admire. I'm sorry that I can't say the same about your scholarship. Tell me, did the Caliph of Baghdad truly threaten to boil you in oil?"

"It was a misunderstanding," Indy said.

"It seems you've had more than your share of misunderstandings," she said. "The professional journals have not treated you kindly. You have the reputation of being something of a—"

"Don't say it," Indy said, wincing. "I know, a grave robber."

"Well," she inquired, "is it true?"

"No," Indy said.

"So all of this grave-robbing business is just another misunderstanding."

"Well, yes."

"It sounds like a convenient excuse," she said. "Tell

me, my misunderstood American, what does all this have to do with Alistair?"

"It's a long story," Indy said. "I would prefer to discuss it with you someplace more private. Could we have lunch somewhere?"

She frowned again.

"I'm sorry, Dr. Jones," she said. "I don't see men socially, and even if I did, it would be quite improper without a chaperon."

"I'm not asking for a date," Indy said irritably. "I need to talk to you about your brother. It's something that could be important to both of us. I'm trying to help, Miss Dunstin, or is the concept unfamiliar to you?"

This time Alecia looked away.

"Yes," she said distantly. "I'm afraid it is."

Indy donned his fedora and walked off.

He was halfway across the reading room when she called to him.

"Dr. Jones," she said, hurrying across the carpeted floor. "Here is the call number of that book you were inquiring after. Sorry to have inconvenienced you."

She extended a slip of paper.

It had an address, and a time—2:00 P.M.—jotted in pencil.

At the windowless and fortresslike Bank of England in the heart of London, Indy was assisted by a dour clerk named Edward Trimbly. Trimbly had been employed by the bank for the past thirty years, and he took pride in the fact that not one farthing had gone astray beneath his keen eye.

"Now, Dr. Jones," Trimbly said. "Some form of

identification will be necessary for us to complete this transaction. Your passport would do nicely."

Indy grinned.

"My passport?" he asked. "I'm afraid I don't have one."

"Oh?" the clerk asked, and his eyebrows went skyward. "How on earth did you get into the country?"

"I came over aboard a U.S. Navy dirigible," he said. "The *Macon.*"

"And were Tinker Bell and Peter Pan aboard?"

"No, really," Indy said. "Well, I didn't actually come all the way to London on the *Macon*. A fighter plane dropped me off at this little airfield out in the country, and from there I took a milk truck into the city. The question of a passport never really came up."

"I see," the clerk said. "No passport. Perhaps a birth certificate, then."

"No birth certificate, either. I dropped everything and left in kind of a hurry."

The clerk chewed his lip.

"All right. A letter, perhaps, on American museum stationery, introducing you to the various authorities on the Isle of Wight with whom you will be working."

Indy shook his head.

"A ticket stub or baggage claim."

"The navy doesn't issue them."

"A business card."

"I don't carry them."

"A note from your mother, perhaps?"

"She's dead," Indy said. "I'm sorry. Was that supposed to be a joke?"

"I'm sorry, Dr. Jones—"

"Call me Indy."

"I'd rather have my tongue gouged out with a spoon," Trimbly said. "There are procedures here which must be followed, despite your American sense of informality. . . . I am almost afraid to ask, Dr. Jones, but what *do* you have?"

Indy searched his pockets and found nothing but lint, then opened his leather satchel. The butt of the Webley revolver protruded prominently.

"Oh, God," the clerk said. "Surely it hasn't come to that."

"It's okay," Indy said. "I'm just looking. Aha!" He found the envelope containing the intelligence files and started to open it. "No, I'm sorry. I can't show you these. Confidential." He replaced the file in the bag.

"Of course," Trimbly said. "The release records from the mental institution, no doubt."

"Surely there must be something." Indy pulled out his wallet. There was the usual accumulation of trash that most Americans carried with them: ticket stubs from the last movie he'd seen, a receipt for dry cleaning, odd notes that he'd scribbled to himself and that now meant nothing. The Boy Scout oath, something he had carried since childhood. A library card.

"Look," Indy said, snatching up the card. "A borrower's card for the Princeton, New Jersey, Free Public Library. See? It has my name typed right on it."

Trimbly examined the card.

"It's expired," he said.

"Oh, come on," Indy pleaded. "If I were going to all the trouble of forging a document, do you think I would pick a *library card*?"

The clerk sighed.

"Would you prefer the amount in pounds or dollars?" Trimbly asked, defeated.

Along with the five hundred dollars that Brody had wired, there was a telegram. INDY: HOPE THIS IS ENOUGH <STOP> ALL I COULD MANAGE ON SHORT NOTICE <STOP> KEEP ME POSTED <STOP> ALL LUCK, BRODY.

"I do hope you drink tea, Dr. Jones."

Alecia Dunstin turned the gas off beneath the whistling kettle and poured two cups of boiling water. The two-bedroom flat in a three-story apartment house on Southampton Row was modest, but clean, and it was just the sort of accommodations that Indy had expected.

"Why did you invite me here?" he asked. "What was all that business about unchaperoned meetings? Did you think I was some kind of masher?"

"One never knows," she said as she placed the tray on the table. "As a matter of fact, I still don't know. But I decided to take a chance. Sugar or cream?"

"Neither, thank you," Indy said. "What made you change your mind?"

"Something about you, I suppose," Alecia said. "That, and what you said about needing someone to talk to. I have been terribly upset since Alistair disappeared, and I am just the sort of person who would pick a rogue like you to confide in."

"A rogue like me?"

"Oh, yes," she said. "Rogues are most effective in this situation. You don't think I would be asking the parson for advice, or perhaps dropping a line to the agony columns?"

"Of course not." Indy cupped the tea in his hands and watched Alecia over the rising steam.

"I visit cemeteries," she said suddenly. "Often I go to Mortlake in the dead of night and visit the grave of Sir Richard. You know of him? He's a distant relative, you know, and my favorite rogue. How I have wished that he could come back—or I could go there—just for a moment."

"What do you mean by go *there*?"

"Back in time, of course. What did you think I meant?"

"Nothing," Indy said. "Tell me about your twin brother."

"Alistair," she said. "We've always been together. We were orphaned at thirteen, when Mum and Dad were killed in an automobile accident. No other kin."

"How old are you now?"

"We're twenty-seven."

"You live together?" Indy asked. There were walking canes in the corner and a brace of pipes on the bookshelf. Across the mantel was a collection of souvenirs: a miniature Eiffel Tower of pot metal, a toy cannon from Gettysburg, a group of lead soldiers, and a curious piece of black obsidian on a wooden stand. Above the mantel was a seventeenth-century blunderbuss, dark with age. "These aren't exactly a woman's touches."

"Yes," Alecia said. "We have been here for years, since Alistair got on at the museum. He's brilliant, you know, but more than a little eccentric."

"I've heard," Indy said. "Did he really make lead into gold?"

Alecia went to the bookshelf and retrieved a matchbox from the pipe rack. She opened it, asked Indy to hold out his hand, and dropped a nugget of gold into his palm.

"Curious," Indy said. "You saw him do this?"

"I helped him," she said.

Her face darkened and her eyes clouded, changing to the color of gunmetal. She forced herself to resist when she saw that Indy had noticed her melancholy.

Indy was about to ask her how she helped him, but he suddenly lost his train of thought.

"Alistair has spent years poring over all those old books and manuscripts," she said quickly. "His room is filled with them. He has a laboratory in the basement, and the landlady, old Mrs. Grundy, is forever complaining—she says it smells like brimstone down there."

"Sulfur," Indy said.

"Yes. It *is* brimstone, come to think of it."

Indy handed back the gold.

"Alistair also keeps pigeons on the roof."

"Pigeons?"

"Yes, passenger pigeons. He breeds them. They are really quite charming. He has pet names for each of them. He belongs to a club—it's really a very popular hobby here in Britain."

"Homing pigeons," Indy said. "The kind they once used to deliver messages."

"I suppose."

"Tell me what Alistair knows about the Voynich Manuscript," Indy said. "I know about its background, how the manuscript was found and so forth. Does Alistair have a theory about what it actually is?"

"He believes that it is much older than anyone suspects," Alecia said. "Not the paper it is written on, or the folio itself, but the secret it contains."

"How old?" Indy asked.

"As old as time itself," Alecia said.

"Come again?"

"We're dealing with very ancient themes here, Dr. Jones. How do you date an idea that has its beginnings in prehistory? As you know, there are various traditions about the founding of alchemy, but most of them have one thing in common. The secret eternal lies hidden in a cave in the desert."

"The Tomb of Hermes," Indy said.

"Yes. Alexander the Great found it and conquered the known world."

"But we're talking about myth," Indy protested. "Nobody takes the Alexander story as fact. It was an invention to explain his affinity with the old gods, a link between the ancient and Hellenistic worlds. Hermes is the divine herald in Greek mythology, a representation of the Egyptian Thoth."

"Also the god of thieves," Alecia said with a smile. "Hermes has taken various forms through the ages, but in alchemical tradition he was a man—Hermes Trismegistus, the thrice great—a contemporary or perhaps even a predecessor of Moses. It wasn't all that long ago that his writings were considered as Christian, and as holy, as the Bible."

"I could argue with you at this point, but I won't. Go on."

"Buried with Hermes is the philosopher's stone, the ultimate repository of alchemical power. The stone reputedly has the ability to transmute elements—turn lead into gold, for instance—and to prolong life indefinitely."

"I'm with you so far," Indy said.

"In the cave, with the stone, was the Emerald Tablet. It gave the basic tenets of alchemy, which emphasize the nearly limitless power of the human mind when coupled with a pure heart. The tablet also contained instructions for making the philosopher's stone."

"Why do you say the tablet *was* there?"

"Because Alexander took it with him," Alecia said. "When Alexander died, the Emerald Tablet was buried with him in his golden sarcophagus at Alexandria."

"So," Indy said, "if Alexander had the secret of immortality, why did he end up as dead as any other mere mortal?"

"It doesn't grant immortality," Alecia said. "It grants *longevity*. It is theoretically possible to live forever, as long as you don't meet with a bullet or a bus. Alexander was poisoned."

Indy nodded.

"Alexandria was the greatest city in the world, the first true center of scholarship and learning. The sages there *knew* the earth was round a thousand years before Columbus did. It was a center for alchemical study and was the location of the world's first great library, but all that knowledge was lost when the city was sacked in the fourth century. The location of Alexander's tomb was lost with it."

Indy finished his tea and placed the cup on the tray.

"This has been an interesting story," he said, "but what does it have to do with the Voynich Manuscript?"

"I'm getting there. You Americans are so bloody impatient. Now we're going to jump ahead a few centuries, to 1357, when a Frenchman named Nicholas Flamel discovers what he calls *The Book of Abraham*, following a dream in which an angel shows him a book in an unrecognizable text."

"Unrecognizable text?"

"Yes, in cipher. Descriptions of this book seem to date it to first-century Alexandria. It consisted of twenty-one pages, with mystical drawings. The last page showed a spring in the desert with serpents issuing from it."

"Serpents?" Indy asked.

"Yes, snakes. The instructions in the book were clear as to how to make the philosopher's stone, but it failed to identify one key ingredient: *prima materia*, the 'first matter' from which the entire process begins."

"Snakes," Indy said.

"In 1382, Flamel—with the help of his wife—was reported to have succeeded in transmutation," Alecia said. "The similarities between *The Book of Abraham* and Voynich are obvious. Then, of course, there is the book that Edward Kelley found in Wales after an angelic dream, which he called *The Gospel of St. Dunstable*. Another mysterious book in an undecipherable text, which probably was the same book that was sold to Rudolph the Second at Prague."

"And all these books, despite the different names, are actually the same?"

Alecia nodded.

"Alchemy is half science and half spiritualism," she said. "The book acts as kind of a Rorschach test for the soul—you look into it long enough, and it mirrors whatever you believe in, whether it is Abraham or St. Dunstable."

"Or Roger Bacon," Indy mused.

"Right," Alecia said. "If you worship empiricism, perhaps you'll see telescopes and microscopes centuries ahead of their time. Poor Newbold."

Indy shook his head.

"But wait a minute," he said. "That's really true of everything, isn't it? You stare at something long enough, and you're going to see more of what's inside you than what that thing really is. Take literary criticism, for example—I have a hunch it tells us far more about the critics than the works they study."

"What about Flamel?" Alecia asked.

"What about him?" Indy retorted. "No offense, but every alchemist worth his medieval salt is reputed to have made a little bit of gold. That comes, no doubt, from some sleight of hand or a clever chemical trick involving gold plating."

"Flamel didn't just make a little," Alecia said. "He made a lot. He and his wife, Perenelle, endowed fourteen hospitals, three chapels, and seven churches. Not a bad record for a charlatan. And it is said they never died. In 1761—when they would have been more than four hundred years old—they were seen attending the opera in Paris."

"Okay," Indy said. "Regardless of whether it's possible to change lead into gold or to live forever, you've convinced me that Voynich may be the same book that has been knocking around Europe for a thousand years, give or take a few centuries. But why would anybody want to go to all the trouble of stealing a book of arcane formulas?"

"That's simple," Alecia said. "The secret it contains is not an obscure alchemical recipe, but the location of the Tomb of Hermes—and the power, perhaps, to conquer the world."

Indy rubbed his jaw.

"What does Alistair want to conquer?" he asked.

"Newtonian physics," Alecia said. "That's all."

"At the museum you said you knew Alistair didn't steal Voynich," Indy said. "That's because you know each other so well?"

Alecia nodded.

"Nobody believes me, of course," she said. "He left for work three days ago and never showed up at the museum. When he came up missing, and Voynich came up missing, they just assumed that he had made off with it. Who else would want it? But they don't know what I know."

"About knowing him so well, you mean."

"That, and something else," Alecia said. Then she hesitated. "Alistair made me promise not to tell anyone else about this. But I'm going to show you so you'll believe me."

She went to the blunderbuss over the mantel. From the barrel she carefully extracted a thick roll of papers. She handed them to Indy. "Why," she asked, "would he steal the bloody thing when he has an exact copy of it?"

"I don't know," Indy said, studying the document. "This is a photographic copy. Perhaps it lacks something vital, such as the coloration of the original."

"You are impossible," Alecia said.

She crossed her arms and stood in front of the window, her back toward Indy. Suddenly Indy remembered that he had wanted to ask her earlier why it took Flamel *and* his wife to transmute gold.

"Alecia—"

"Dr. Jones," she said. "Are you expecting visitors?"

The door to the apartment burst inward, knocked from its latch by a booted foot. Luigi Volatore—the last of the brothers—strode into the room behind the barrel of a Mauser, followed by two *atlantici.*

"Search the apartment," he snapped in Italian. "Find them."

The pair went from room to room, looking in closets and beneath beds, sometimes kicking over furniture in frustration, but the apartment was empty.

Luigi cursed.

He picked up one of the cups from the table near the sofa. He sipped the tea. It was still warm. Then he walked to the open window and looked out on Southampton Row. The street was empty. He closed the window with a bang.

"They can't be far," he said. "Tear the place apart. Take anything that Sarducci might have the slightest interest in."

The pair began emptying drawers and sifting through the accumulating pile of papers. They stuffed anything that looked official into a suitcase they had taken from a bedroom.

"We will leave a surprise for them, I think." Luigi walked to a writing desk by the wall and, from a cup that bristled with pencils and rubber bands, picked out a shiny paper clip.

While the others worked he examined the gas line that ran to the burners behind a ceramic heating grate in the fireplace. Nodding, he went to the switch on the wall next to the front door and thumbed it, satisfying himself that there was current flowing to the light fixture overhead. He turned the switch back and the light died. He put the paper clip between his teeth. Standing on a chair, he used a butcher knife to cut the light fixture from the wires. He tossed the fixture in a corner of the room, where it shattered.

He hummed an aria as he worked.

He took the paper clip from his mouth and stretched it out, then twisted each end around the wires above the insulation. He manipulated the paper clip until the bare copper ends hung close together, not quite touching.

Luigi admired his handiwork and stepped down from the chair.

"Hurry," he told the other two.

He went to the kitchen, blew out the pilot lights, and cranked open all of the gas valves on the burners. With a snakelike hiss, the explosive gas began to fill the apartment. Then he went back to the fireplace and drove his heel into the gas line there until it finally snapped free of its connection.

"Time to go," he said.

The pair latched the suitcase.

They went out the open door ahead of Luigi, who turned for one last look at the apartment. He took a cigar from his breast pocket and stuck it in the corner of his mouth. Then he laughed and pulled the door shut, wedging it in place against the broken latch.

Standing on the ledge outside the apartment, three stories above the sidewalk, Indy felt the ache in his fingers as they clutched the rough stonework.

Alecia's arms were around his waist.

"Are they gone?" she asked.

"I think so," Indy said. "I heard the door slam. We have to find a way to get back inside before they hit the sidewalk and see us perched up here. Does the window latch from the inside?"

"Yes," Alecia said.

"We don't have time to pry it open," he said. "Is the window on the other side of you up?"

"A bit," she said.

"Edge your way over to it."

"I'm afraid to move," she said.

"Be more afraid of those guns," Indy said.

Alecia crept along the ledge, a baby step at a time, until she was near enough the window to reach inside. The window was open only a few inches, and she reached to raise it. The ledge gave way beneath her and she fell, but caught herself on the sill.

Indy grasped her arm and pulled her up. When she had regained her footing, he opened the window and she stepped inside. As he followed her into the next-door apartment he saw the top of Luigi's head on the sidewalk below.

"Sorry," Alecia told the shocked couple who were eating toast and listening to the BBC. "We were feeding the pigeons and locked ourselves out."

"No problem," the man said. "I've done it myself."

"You have not," the woman said. "Why do you always lie? Pay no attention to the old fool," she said, and made a swirling motion beside her head. "Would you care for some toast and jam?"

"It looks delicious," Alecia said politely, "but no, thank you. Don't mind us, we'll let ourselves out."

They raced down the hall and Alecia fumbled with her keys.

"You won't need those," Indy said, observing the broken door frame. He pushed the door open and they stepped into the shadowy apartment. Alecia reached for the light switch.

Indy grabbed her wrist.

"Don't," he said, and nodded toward the bare wires hanging overhead where the light fixture had been. "The apartment is filled with natural gas."

Indy took a deep breath and stepped into the room. He crossed over the pile of discarded papers and went to the fireplace, where he knelt at the hearth and examined the severed line. He closed the valve and the hissing stopped. Then he went to the kitchen and turned off the burners there. By the time he came back to the front door, he was light-headed and his lungs burned for air.

"They've ransacked the apartment," he said, gasping.

Alecia nodded. Her lips were tight. She was sweating, and she put her head forward, gathered her mane of red hair, and lifted it from the back of her neck. Indy was momentarily distracted by the graceful curve of her neck, and her finely sculpted, almost elflike ears. He also glimpsed, on the nape of her neck, a small but intricate design of interlocking red-and-black circles. The tattoo began just beneath the hairline and wound down her neck to disappear beneath the fabric of her blouse. The pattern, Indy realized, was Celtic. When she saw him looking, she released her hair and let it fall back into place.

"What now?" she asked.

"They will be expecting an explosion," Indy said. "They'll be watching from somewhere along the street below."

"Then they will return," Alecia said.

Indy nodded.

"I thought I had a few more days, because the armada is still in the middle of the Atlantic. They must have radioed ahead."

She took a deep breath and entered the apartment. She gathered her purse from the floor. Then she went to the fireplace. With her back to Indy, she took the chunk of obsidian from the mantel and placed it in her purse. Then she fished the photographic copy of the Voynich Manuscript from the muzzle of the blunderbuss. When she returned she handed it to Indy.

He placed it in his satchel.

"Where do we go now?" she asked.

"We?" he asked. "*I* am on my way to Rome. You should find yourself someplace safe to hide. Relatives in the country, perhaps."

"I have no other relatives besides Alistair," she said. "We must go together."

"It's too dangerous."

Alecia's eyes narrowed.

"This was my apartment they just tried to blow up," she said. "We are partners in this whether you like it or not. I will go with you to Rome."

Indy hesitated. She came close to him and grasped his arm. Her lips brushed his.

"You need me, Dr. Jones."

"Now, wait a minute—"

"You can't read Voynich," she said. "But *I* can. Alistair showed me how. It's very simple, really, once you get the hang of it. And once you have *this.*"

She removed the chunk of obsidian from her purse.

"The Shew Stone," Indy said.

They hurried down the stairs and left the apartment building by the back entrance, then followed the winding alley for block after block. Indy thought once that they had been followed, but after waiting for a quarter of an hour in a dark alcove, he could detect nothing.

"We're safe," Alecia said. "There's nobody back there."

"Maybe," Indy said, stepping out into the light. He rubbed his eyes. "Look, I haven't eaten today. I need some food. Is there someplace close?"

"There's a pub just around the corner," she said.

"You know where we are?" he asked. "This looks like a pretty rough part of town."

"This is London, Dr. Jones," she said. "There's a pub around every corner."

The predicted establishment was found beneath the sign of the Dark Horse. They sat in rough wooden pews and drank pints of warm beer and endured the un-abashedly curious—and occasionally hostile—gazes of the workingmen while waiting for Indy's meal to arrive.

"I feel like we're in a fishbowl," Indy said.

"Not us," Alecia said, wiping the beer foam from the corner of her mouth with the back of her hand. "Just you."

"You've been here before?"

"Never," she said. "But I fit. You don't. They're very protective of their turf, and they don't like outsiders."

"Terrific."

"You said you wanted food."

"I'd also like to keep some teeth to eat it with," Indy said.

"Don't be such a baby," Alecia said. She smiled knowingly toward the brooding men at the bar, as if they were sharing some private joke. While she had managed to establish some unspoken understanding with the rest of them, a particularly rough-looking fellow in a frayed wool sweater and gray cap continued to scowl.

"There was something I'm curious about," Indy said.

"More questions?" Alecia asked.

"Yes. Why did it take both Flamel and his wife to transmute gold?" Indy paused while his steaming plate of meat and potatoes was deposited before him by a barmaid who seemed as displeased by his presence as the others were. "Couldn't he do it by himself?"

"That's difficult to answer," Alecia said carefully.

Indy stabbed at the meat with his fork.

"You need to know much more about alchemy before you can begin to understand it," she said.

"Try me," Indy said, although his attention seemed to be focused on his food.

"All right," she said. "But you need to look at me, Dr. Jones."

Their eyes met.

"No," he said, glancing away. "I'm not going to let you do the trick with your eyes again. I want an answer —although I think I already know what it is. The transmutation requires the help of a *soror mystica*, doesn't it?"

Alecia's face reddened.

"I thought so," Indy said. "Talk to me, sister."

The man in the gray cap slammed his beer down on the bar. He lumbered over, crossed his arms, and stood with his feet planted squarely on the floor. He weighed a good two hundred and fifty pounds, and although the buttons of his sweater looked as if they were about to pop over his big belly, there was plenty of real muscle on his arms and shoulders; Indy judged him for a black-smith, and his fists looked the size of anvils.

"This Yank bothering you, miss?" the big man asked.

"No," Alecia said. "Thank you for asking, though."

"I don't like Yanks," the man said. "Especially ones that refuse to remove their hats in the presence of ladies. I've half a mind to thrash you."

"Sorry, friend," Indy said. He placed the fedora on the table and smiled. "Is this better?"

"Apologize to the lady."

"Okay," Indy said. "Miss Dunstin, I apologize. Are we through?"

"Not quite," the man said. "I don't like your lop-sided grin. I think I'll thrash you anyway."

"Well, you're right about one thing," Indy said. "Half a mind is all you've got."

The man grabbed Indy by the collar and pulled him from the pew as easily as if he were handling a sack of potatoes. Indy drew his fist, but before he could land a punch, Alecia clapped her hands together and began talking rapidly in a language that vaguely resembled Romanian, but that Indy didn't understand.

The big man looked sheepish. He released his hold, and Indy fell to the floor. He doffed his cap and spoke briefly to Alecia in the unknown language.

"Sorry," he told Indy before returning to the bar.

"What on earth did you say to him?" Indy asked, picking himself up and dusting off his clothes. "And in what language? I've never heard it before."

"It is Shelta Thari," Alecia said. "Tinker's talk. It is the old language of the Celts, and it is used by those who know the secrets of metal."

"It's related to the tattoo on the back of your neck, isn't it?"

"Yes," she said.

"You haven't told me everything," Indy said.

Alecia looked away.

"You're more than Alistair's sister, aren't you?" Indy asked, leaning over the table. "You're his *soror mystica.* Alistair needs you—he can't transmute gold by himself. Not that I believe in any of this malarkey, of course. And you're the one who can read the manuscript, not him. For all I know, you're up to your pretty, tattooed neck in this thing. Maybe Sarducci's thugs were trying to kill both of us—but then again, maybe they were just trying to kill *me.* They need you."

Alecia shook her head. She looked deeply into his eyes.

"Dr. Jones, you must believe me," she said.

Indy looked away.

"No," he said, "I don't. But the real question is what *you* believe in, Miss Dunstin."

"My allegiance is to Alistair."

"And what about *his* allegiance?" Indy asked.

Alecia bit her lower lip.

"I don't know," she said. "I don't blame you for not trusting me. You're right, I haven't told you everything. But it's not because I wanted to deceive you in any way. I . . . well, I was afraid you would think less of me. I have done some things in my life that I'm not exactly proud of. Alistair and I are not like normal people, you know. It's a curse that we've carried since we were children."

Indy speared a chunk of potato and placed it in his mouth. It was delicious. He followed it with a slice of meat. Warmth filled his stomach, and he could feel his strength slowly returning.

"It's difficult to explain," Alecia said.

"I'm a good listener," Indy said.

"The tattoo," she said. "I've had it since I was seven years old. It starts at the back of my neck, spreads across my shoulder blades and down my spine to the small of my back."

"A kell?" Indy asked.

"Not exactly," she said. "It is the mark of the Thari, the ancient Druid caste of metalworkers, from the time when the knowledge of working metal into swords was more magic than science. Shelta Thari is the secret language of the bards, the priests, and the magicians, and it is a very old language—prehistoric, perhaps, going all the way back to the Bronze Age. Alistair and I are the survivors of a dying race."

"The man that wanted to thrash me," Indy said. "A blacksmith?"

"Yes," Alecia said. "The language survives, mostly among blacksmiths and beggars and Gypsies who know a few key phrases. *Nus a dhabjan dhuilsa,* for example. 'The blessing of God upon you.' Some scholars have attempted to transcribe the language, but none have succeeded. It is the habit of the Thari to either deny its existence, or to provide gibberish to those who inquire."

"I'll remember that."

"When our parents died, the Thari provided for Alistair and me," she said. "They told us, in fact, that we are of royal blood, that I am the last—well, *priestess.*"

"And Alistair?" Indy asked. "Is he a priest of some sort? Does he have a tattoo on his back as well?"

"No." Alecia laughed. "Thari is a very . . . matriarchal society. Our mother was—" She stopped. She was gazing across Indy's shoulder.

"Is something wrong?"

"Don't turn around," Alecia said. "Those men again. Three of them. The one with the cigar seems to be the leader."

"What are they doing?"

"They are standing just inside the doorway," Alecia said. "Their eyes haven't adjusted yet from the sunlight. They are looking over the pub. We must leave."

"The back door," Indy said.

He stood, and pulled a roll of bills from his pocket. He fumbled with the pound notes, not knowing how much to leave. Alecia reached over and pulled a five-pound note from the roll and left it on the table.

"Too much, I know. But it's for the damages."

"What damages?" Indy asked.

Alecia walked to the bar and spoke briefly in Shelta to the blacksmith. He nodded. Then she grasped Indy's hand and pulled him toward the back room.

One of the *atlantici* spotted them.

"Stop!" he shouted, and began hurrying toward them.

As he passed the bar the blacksmith turned and punched the man squarely in the face. He went sprawling backward into a table, spilling beer over the customers sitting there. One of them picked him up from the floor and backhanded him, sending him reeling back toward the bar.

Indy heard glasses breaking and the unmistakable sounds of fists smacking into flesh as he and Alecia threaded their way through the kitchen. The back door was locked. Indy hunched his shoulder and made a run at the stout wooden door. It budged not at all.

"Americans," Alecia said with a snort. "Here, let me try."

"Be my guest," Indy said, rubbing his shoulder.

Alecia ran her hand along the top of the door frame and found the key that was hidden there. She inserted it into the lock, which turned easily, and then she swung the door open.

"Jeesh," Indy said.

They emerged into a narrow alley.

Indy blinked hard against the sunlight.

They turned to follow the alley to the street, but they had gone no more than a few steps when the trio of men in dark uniforms appeared at the corner. Behind them was a dead end; the alley ended in a soot-blackened brick wall.

The men began to walk with careful deliberation toward them. One of them, Luigi, was smoking a cigar. The other two produced guns from beneath their coats.

"That was quick," Indy said.

"Now what?" Alecia asked.

Indy pulled her toward the wooden fence lining the back of the alley. He scrambled up a stack of garbage cans, balancing precariously on top as a stray cat screamed and bared its teeth before darting away. Alecia looped the strap of her purse around her head and shoulder so she wouldn't lose it. Indy pulled her up behind him, then begged her pardon as he planted his right hand on her bottom and boosted her to the top of the fence. Then he pulled himself up.

"You there!" an English voice shouted. "Stop!"

Indy and Alecia paused for a moment atop the

wooden fence. A policeman was at the mouth of the alley, and he blew three shrill notes on his whistle.

"Good," Indy said.

Alecia shook her head.

"He doesn't have a gun. No bobby does," she said.

The trio of dark men turned slowly, their gun barrels pointing in the air, and they regarded the policeman with contempt. The whistle dropped from the bobby's mouth and hung from the end of the silver chain at his waist.

The bobby hesitated, then ran.

Indy and Alecia dropped to the muddy ground on the other side of the fence. They were in the back lot of a scrap dealer, amid piles of rusting engine blocks and crumpled sheet metal. A pyramid of discarded oil and petrol drums stood near the fence.

"If we live through this," Indy said, "we go our separate ways. Agreed?"

"Agreed," Alecia said. "But which way now?"

The rattle of the garbage cans announced that the dark men would soon be over the fence.

"There," Indy said, pointing to the rusting hulk of a bulldozer planted in the middle of the lot, its blade facing the fence. Alecia ran for cover while he pulled the revolver from his satchel and backed away from the fence. Indy sent a round over the top of the first head that popped above the weathered planks. The bullet smacked impotently against the brick wall of the pub building. Alarmed by the report, dogs began to howl for blocks around.

Indy smiled and walked toward the dozer.

"Indy!" Alecia screamed. "Are you crazy? You can't start a gun battle in the middle of London!"

Indy shrugged.

"*They've* got guns," he said. "Besides, they wouldn't da—"

Indy lunged for safety as the chatter of a machine pistol erupted from atop the fence. He and Alecia crouched low as the heavy slugs beat a deafening staccato against the heavy blade.

Indy shook his head and tugged at his ears.

"Wouldn't dare, huh?" Alecia fumed.

"What?" Indy asked.

"I said you were a pigheaded, shortsighted, American jerk!"

"What?" Indy asked.

Another burst slammed against the blade.

"They'll finish us before help can reach us," Indy said.

Alecia's eyes burned with anger.

"Who can stop them?" Indy asked. "I have five shots left, and they have—what?—a couple of hundred, perhaps."

"I'm calling you stupid," she shouted. "Dumb. Get it? Dumb!"

"Drums," Indy said. His eyes flashed. "Think anything is left in 'em?"

Indy dove around the end of the blade and sent two rounds into the heap of discarded drums, then jerked back as the machine pistol answered.

"Nothing," he muttered. "They can't *all* be empty, can they?"

"What?" Alecia asked.

Indy waited until the salvo stopped, then took a deep breath.

He popped over the top and fired once more.

Nothing happened.

"I'm sorry," Indy said. "They've got us. I only have two rounds left. When I give you the signal, run like hell. I can only hold them off for a few seconds."

Alecia seized him by his leather jacket, pulled him roughly toward her, and kissed him firmly on the lips. Her mouth was warm and moist, and he could smell her perfume—it reminded him of honeysuckle—mixed with sweat and fear. Indy nearly dropped his gun.

Then she released him.

"I'll stay with you," she said.

The man with the cigar mounted the fence. His companions, the ones with the machine pistols, were already on the ground. He motioned for them to advance, to finish it quickly before help could arrive.

Luigi took one last puff on the cigar, then absentmindedly flicked it away. He froze as he realized his mistake, then he watched as the trajectory of the glowing butt carried it—as if in slow motion—into a puddle beside a leaking petrol drum.

Luigi dropped back behind the fence.

The mountain of drums exploded with a dull thud, engulfing the men with the machine pistols in a blackveined blossom of orange flame. As Indy ducked he could feel the heat of the explosion wash over the top of the bulldozer blade.

Alecia's eyes were wide with terror.

"Keep your head down," Indy said. "Move out—now!"

They threaded their way around the piles of scrap to the front of the yard, where Indy used a short length of pipe he found on the ground to snap the chain that held the gate. The fire burned brightly behind them—

but seemed to be contained within the back part of the yard—as the scream of sirens approached.

Indy paused for a moment before opening the gate.

"I guess this is good-bye. You have to go," he said.

"I guess so," Alecia said uncomfortably.

"Unless . . ." Indy ventured.

"No," Alecia said. "It's better this way. What happened back there—"

"The kiss—"

"Right," she said, brushing the hair away from her eyes. She was uncomfortably aware of the weight of the Shew Stone in her purse. "Look, it didn't mean anything. It was impulsive, foolish. Forget it."

"Right," Indy said.

He opened his satchel. "You'll want your copy of Voynich."

"No," she said. "Take it. You'll need it."

He opened the gate.

They emerged beneath a hand-painted sign, which neither of them saw. It warned: JONES WRECKING—NO TRESPASSING—ENTER AT YOUR OWN RISK.

Indy turned toward the east while Alecia hesitated a moment, staring longingly at his back. Her face was warmed by more than the fire in the scrap yard. Indy's steps did not slow, and he did not look back. Alecia shouldered her purse, turned on her heel, and walked toward the west.

A fire truck raced past.

"Bloody Yank," she said softly.

She paused at the corner, unsure of which way to turn. Going back to the apartment was out of the question, and she couldn't return to work at the British Museum—it would be too easy for the fascists to find her there. But they would find her eventually, she decided, wherever she went. Her only choice, she concluded, was to go where she was least expected: Rome. There, at least, she could continue her search for Alistair.

She turned toward the Thames.

5

FLOTSAM AND JETSAM

The lights of London slid slowly past while the garbage boat continued its methodical journey to the sea. The sun had dipped below the horizon a quarter of an hour before, leaving the western sky smudged with gold, and the Thames resembled a dull sheet of lead. Sitting at the stern of the boat, watching the city recede in the distance, Alecia shuddered.

"You cold, miss?" the captain asked. He had a dark wool coat in his weathered hands.

"Thank you," Alecia said.

The skipper draped the coat around her shoulders.

"I'm afraid we haven't much to eat on the *Mary Reilly*," he said. "But you're welcome to what we have. Coffee, bread. Some cheese."

Alecia nodded.

"I'm sure it's none of my business, but if you don't mind my asking, what are you afraid of back there? Are

you running away from something? Is somebody following you?"

"Something like that," Alecia said.

"A man, I'll bet," the skipper said. He made a
sound in his throat. "I've got three daughters myself,
and I understand. Seems as if the good Lord is punish-
ing me for the transgressions of my youth."

Alecia smiled.

"Life will go on," the skipper said gently. He patted
her on the shoulder. "I'll be up in the wheelhouse if you
need anything. Don't worry, miss—it doesn't matter
what you're running from, or to. You're safe while you're
on my command. Even if she is only a garbage scow."

"I'm sure of it," Alecia said.

A pair of running lights on the river grew closer,
and as they did she could hear the insectlike drone of an
outboard motor laboring at top speed. Alecia went to the
wheelhouse.

"Are you expecting anyone?" she asked the skipper.

"No," he said.

"Is there someplace to hide?"

"Not to worry," the man said. "I won't let anything
happen to you."

"You don't know the kind of people I've been dealing with lately," she said. "They'll kill you."

The skipper made the sound deep in his throat
again. Without taking his left hand from the wheel, he
reached to a box on the wall and withdrew a revolver.
He slipped the gun in his pocket.

The motorboat pulled alongside and throttled back
its engine.

"Snopes," he called. "Forget those lines for now.
Get up here and take the wheel."

The skipper relinquished the vessel to his first—and only—mate. He gave Alecia a reassuring smile and said, "You'd better stay here, miss."

A man leaped from the deck of the motorboat onto the *Mary Reilly*. He nearly lost his hat, but caught it before it went into the dirty river water.

"You'd better get right back where you came from, son." The skipper motioned with the barrel of the gun. "She doesn't want to see you."

"Jones!" Alecia called from the wheelhouse.

Indy smiled and held his hands palms out.

"It's all right, skipper," Alecia said. She came down from the wheelhouse.

"You want him here?"

"This is not one of the men I'm afraid of," Alecia said. "Well, not very much, anyway. Please let him stay."

Indy grinned and waved at the motorboat. It swung away, leaving a shimmering wake as it turned back toward London.

"Now look here," the skipper said. "I'm not running some bloody passenger line for indigents. I was glad enough to take the young miss, but—"

"I can pay," Indy said.

The skipper cleared his throat.

"Well, that's different."

"Jones," Alecia said. She put her arms around his waist and hugged him. "You changed your mind. I never thought I'd see you again. How did you find me?"

Indy's grin turned sheepish.

"I need you," he said.

"Oh no," Alecia said. She released him and backed away. "You bastard. You bloody followed me, didn't you?"

"I couldn't let you go off alone," Indy said. "I had to make sure *you* weren't being followed. Besides, I need you to help me find Alistair."

"That's why you need me?" she asked. "That's all there is to it? You left me on the sidewalk feeling like a piece of chewing gum that you had scraped from the bottom of your shoe, and now you show up here because you need my help?"

"But you said to forget about—"

"And you believed me?"

"Well—"

The skipper stepped between them.

"Do you want me to put him in the drink, miss?" the skipper asked. "He looks healthy enough. He could swim to shore from here."

"Yes," Alecia said. "Throw him overboard like some of this stinking garbage."

"Alecia," Indy pleaded. He looked longingly for the motorboat, but it was out of sight.

"No," she said. "Don't. That's too good for him. You let me deal with him—that will be punishment enough. The fact is I need him, too, to help me find my brother. It will be a business arrangement from now on, do you understand, Dr. Jones?"

"I thought that was all—"

"Oh, shut up," Alecia said, and walked away.

The skipper put the gun back in his pocket.

"You'd better pay me now, son," he said. "I don't know how long you'll be with us."

Indy placed the copy of the Voynich Manuscript on the table in the tiny cabin belowdecks. He removed the rub-

ber band from around his notebook, spread the pages
flat, and sharpened his pencil with a pocketknife.

Alecia came down the stairs but stopped when she
saw Indy.

"I'm sorry," she said. "I'll let you be. I was just
looking for the water closet."

"There isn't one," Indy said. "I already asked."

"Then . . ."

"Over the side," Indy said.

Alecia wrinkled her nose.

"Nothing that can't wait," she said philosophically.
"What are you doing?"

"Looking for clues," Indy said.

"You can't read it," Alecia said condescendingly.

"I know, but there might be something in the drawings."

"Do you want some help?"

"You're offering?"

"This is a professional arrangement," she said
coolly. "I'm willing to do my share."

"Good," Indy said. "Have a seat. Perhaps you
wouldn't mind telling me what all of this means. You did
help Alistair decipher some of it, didn't you?"

"I don't remember anything about it," she said. "I
mean, when I scryed—when I helped him to translate it
—I was in a sort of trance. He's the one who kept the
transcription. I haven't the foggiest notion of anything I
said."

Indy sighed.

"What about the drawings?"

Alecia leafed through the pages.

"I'm sorry," she said. "They don't mean anything to

me. The manuscript itself, of course, is in color. That could be part of the cipher."

"I've thought of that," Indy said. "We're at a disadvantage because we don't have the original. Still, we have to try. There has to be some way to wring some meaning from all of this."

Alecia nodded. She took the Shew Stone from her purse and placed it on the table.

"What are you doing?"

"Well, you said we had to try. So I'm willing. If it worked with Alistair, I might be able to do it alone."

"I have to tell you, Alecia, that this all reminds me of that business with Arthur Conan Doyle and the fairies," Indy said.

"You don't have to believe in it," Alecia said, "you just have to take notes. Besides, you're just saying that to protect your image as a scientist—I think you actually believe in it quite a bit, Dr. Jones, but you're not willing to admit it."

Indy shook his head.

"Parlor games," he said. "But help yourself."

Alecia placed the Shew Stone on the copy of the manuscript. She cleared her throat, brushed her hair back with her hands, and took a deep breath. She let it out slowly while staring at the Shew Stone.

"Do you have enough light?"

Alecia sighed and closed her eyes.

"I need you to be quiet," she said.

She tilted her head down, opened her eyes again, and stared at the lump of obsidian. Nothing seemed to happen for the first ten minutes. Then her brow, which had been furrowed with concentration, began to relax. Her breathing became slower and more regular, her eyes turned dull and unfocused. She bent lower over the copy. Her hair fell about her face, and her right hand moved the Shew Stone over the lines of cipher.

Praise be to God for perpetually bestowing upon us His gifts. After this follow our prayers for the prophet Abraham and his family, to whom this book is humbly dedicated. Peace be upon them!

Indy was startled. Alecia was speaking with the voice of a man, a very old man. He took up his pencil and began to write.

Here is the account of al-Jabir ibn-Hayyan, to expound the wisdom which was revealed to me after I left the Tomb of Hermes and took hold of the Tabula Smaragdina. I declare: Those who enter the cave and are not pure of heart shall sicken and die within a fortnight, and those who are reckless in the opening of the golden cask containing the Stone shall be smitten according to where they stand.

Indy began to write faster.

Here are the revelations of Hermes:

Speak not fictitious things, but that which is certain and true; what is below is like that which is above, and what is above is like that which is below.

As all things were produced by the one word of God, so all things are produced from this one thing by adaptation; seek the prima materia, *for thus you will obtain the glory of the whole world, and obscurity will shun you. It is the first path to the Stone.*

It was forged by fire, borne by water, brought down from the sky by wind, and nourished by the earth. It is in every place; housewives cast it out, children play with it.

Be free from all ambition, hypocrisy, and vice; a wicked man shall never succeed.

Alecia's head bobbed forward, and she swayed in her chair.

Indy dropped his pencil. Using both hands, he reached across the table and grasped her by the shoulders. Her eyes fluttered open. She looked around, momentarily confused. Then she swallowed and sat upright.

"I'm fine," she said.

"You don't look fine," Indy said.

"I am," she said. "Did you get anything?"

"Yes." Indy pushed the notebook across to her. "But I'm afraid it raises more questions than it answers."

She turned the pages of the notebook.

"Your handwriting is atrocious," Alecia said. "What do they teach in America? I need you to decipher. What's this word here?"

"I was in a hurry," Indy said defensively. He peered at the line where her finger rested. "*Prima materia.* That's 'first matter.'"

"Oh, two words," Alecia said. "I couldn't tell. And this?"

Indy looked again.

"Tabula Smaragdina," he said.

"The Emerald Tablet," she said.

Alecia leaned back in her chair.

"This al-Jabir," Alecia said. "If memory serves, he is the Arab mystic and mathematician from whom we get modern algebra, is he not?"

"Yes," Indy said. "But his name also serves as the Latin root of our word *gibberish.* And that's what we seem to have here—a list of meaningless riddles."

Alecia pushed herself away from the table.

"I'm exhausted," she said. "If you don't mind, I'm

going to stretch out for a bit. Please wake me before we get to the channel. That's where they'll dump their garbage, and we have to find another boat before then."

Alecia lay down on the bunk alongside the opposite wall. In a moment she was asleep. Indy found a tattered blanket in the compartment above and spread it over her. He returned to the table, thumbed listlessly through the transcription, then put the notebook down.

He watched Alecia as she slept.

Indy picked up his pencil and began to sketch on a blank page in the notebook. It was Alecia, with her hair spilling about her head, her lips slightly parted, her features relaxed. He paid particular attention to her ears— they were finely sculpted and seemed to come to the faintest suggestion of a point—and her delicate, upturned nose.

Her heart-shaped face seemed particularly childlike now. He wanted to believe her story. It was easy to imagine her as seven years old, being told that she was the last of a special race, being admonished to lie still while facedown on a table in some tattoo parlor as needles pricked a centuries-old design into her skin. Still, Indy could not think of the tattoo as disfiguring her; in fact, what he had spied of it just added to her beauty. He wanted to see the rest of the tattoo. He imagined he saw it unfold across her bare back like a pair of delicate wings.

He put the pencil down and rubbed his eyes.

Although he did not trust her, Indy realized, he was starting to care for her. He rested his head on his folded arms and slipped into a deep, dreamless sleep.

· · ·

Indy woke to the thud of boots upon the deck, followed by the sound of angry voices. He scooped up his notebook and copies of the manuscript and placed them in his satchel, along with half a box of .38-caliber shells— the skipper's gun took the same cartridge as the Webley —from a shelf in the cabin. Then he knelt beside Alecia and shook her awake.

"Are we there?" she asked groggily.

"Quiet," Indy said. "We have company."

Indy took her by the hand and pulled her up the steps to the doorway of the cabin. It was still dark out, but he could see the beam of flashlights playing over the bow. Forward, the skipper was arguing with a group of soldiers. He could hear the old man's voice rise with anger, demanding to know why his boat had been boarded. Two men grasped his arms from behind while a third shoved the ends of a wool scarf into his mouth. Behind them, outlined by its running lights, was the familiar shape of a double-hulled flying boat resting silently on the water.

"How did they find us?" Alecia asked.

"I don't know," Indy said. "But we've got to hide."

"Where? You couldn't hide a Yorkshire terrier on a boat this size. If they've got us, we might as well fight it out with them now. Make a stand of it."

"Come on, Princess," Indy said as he grabbed his hat and pulled her out of the cabin. "I'm not ready to make my last stand yet. If it's between Custer and the Indians, I'll side with the Indians."

"Search the boat," Luigi said, motioning painfully with his bandaged hands. The half-dozen *atlantici* fanned out, threading their way between the heaps of garbage to the cabin. "We know they're here. Be careful—the American is armed, although he is rather a bad shot."

"With your cigars," Sarducci said, "it seems he didn't need to be accurate."

Luigi shrugged.

"I was meaning to give them up, anyway."

"Are you sure the motorboat owner told you the truth?"

"Dying declarations usually are true," Luigi said.

The skipper closed his eyes while the soldiers clambered into the boat's only cabin.

"The cabin's empty," one of the soldiers called back in Italian. "But we found this." He held up Alecia's purse.

"Bring it here," Sarducci said.

"So no women are aboard your boat, eh?" Luigi asked. "I suppose you always take your purse when you go to sea. I wonder what else you might be carrying." Luigi searched his pockets and found the gun.

"Expecting trouble?" he asked, clumsily breaking open the revolver with his bandaged hands and regarding the six shining brass cases.

Sarducci inspected the purse.

"Ah, but I hate the trash that women carry in these things," he said, flinging lipstick and rouge and a hairbrush overboard. "This, now, is something else." He retrieved the Shew Stone and held it aloft. "They are here."

Luigi snapped the cylinder of the revolver back with a flourish. Then he leaned close to the old man's face. "You lied to me. I despise liars."

Luigi whipped the barrel of the gun across the skipper's face, hard enough so that the men holding him nearly fell backward. Snopes, who was struggling with his captors in the wheelhouse, gave up when the barrel of a machine gun was pressed against the small of his back.

Luigi pulled the scarf from the skipper's mouth. The old man continued to stare defiantly at him, despite the blood running between his eyes.

"Where are they?" Luigi asked.

The skipper was silent.

"Search the rest of this stinking excuse for a boat," Luigi ordered in Italian. "They are here somewhere. Be careful not to hurt the girl. We need her untouched. When you find the American, bring him to me—I want to kill him myself, out of respect for my brothers."

Ten minutes later the soldiers had searched every inch above- and belowdecks. Luigi began pacing and barking orders to the men to search the ship again.

"Calm yourself," Sarducci said. "We haven't searched everywhere, not yet. There's one other place that they could be—the most obvious place, really."

"What do you mean?" Luigi asked. "There is nowhere else—ah, the garbage. But there are mountains of it. Are we to sift through every rotting pile?"

Sarducci turned to the skipper.

"You dump the garbage here in the channel, no? Then proceed with your business."

The old man shook his head.

"See?" Sarducci told Luigi. "I am right. But then, I am always right, am I not? The man in the wheelhouse —tell him to dump the garbage, or he will become a part of it."

"But the girl," Luigi protested. "We are not to touch her."

"We do our best," Sarducci said. "But Jones must die. If he takes the girl with him, then how are we to prevent that? Besides, if we can recover the body, then that is all we need. Tell him to dump the garbage."

Snopes refused.

The gun barrel was shoved harder into his back. He heard the click of the safety being switched off.

"One other thing," Sarducci said. "Start the engine and engage the propeller, won't you? A slow idle should be sufficient. Make a wide circle around our aircraft."

"Skipper?" Snopes called.

"Go ahead," the old man called. "God will understand."

Snopes pushed the starter button, and the diesel rumbled to life. Then he threw the lever for hold number one, causing the hydraulic doors on deck to swing inward. Tons of refuse showered down into the cold channel sea, amid the shriek of a chorus of rodents.

The *atlantici* looked down into the water, their machine guns poised. A cloud of roiling garbage blossomed at the stern, behind the propellers.

"Anything?" Sarducci called.

"Only rats," came the answer. "Lots of rats."

"Now the others," Sarducci called.

Snopes crossed himself and tripped the remaining two levers.

In the third hold, beneath a pile of coffee grounds and eggshells and newspapers that had once wrapped fish and chips and a hundred other things that smelled even worse, Indy held Alecia tight against him as she struggled.

"We're going to drown," she gasped.

"No, we're not," he said. He kicked a rat away from his ankle. "Relax. Save your strength."

Their mound of trash bounced as hold number two gave way and dropped its load into the sea.

"When we hit the water, swim down and out as far as you can, to get clear of the screws. Then come up on the other side. That's the plan."

"You call that a plan?" Alecia asked. "I can't swim!"

"Oh," Indy said as the doors beneath them groaned. He grasped Alecia's hand tightly. "That changes things. Take a deep breath, and don't fight—"

Suddenly they were plummeting downward with the trash. The channel was freezing. Indy forced his eyes open against the stinging water, but could see nothing. He could feel, however, dozens of rats clawing the water around them.

He released his grip on Alecia's hand and spun her around in the water, then grasped her beneath the arms with his left hand and held her tight against him.

Indy dove as deeply as he could with his burden, kicking hard with his legs, using his free hand to help pull them through the water. Alecia writhed and clawed at his hand, but he wouldn't let go. He swam until he thought his lungs would burst, then he forced himself to swim even more. His ears began to ring and streaks of lightning seemed to explode in his head.

Suddenly he was unsure which way was up and which was down. He was out of breath, the freezing water was beginning to stiffen his muscles, his lungs were on fire, and he could not tell which way to swim for the surface.

He blew the last of the air out of his used-up lungs.

The bubbles shot upward, and as they brushed against his cheek he knew in which direction to swim.

They broke the surface of the water and Indy gratefully filled his lungs with night air. Alecia gasped, gulped down as much water as air, choked. After she had gained her breath, but before she could scream, Indy planted a hand over her mouth and shook his head. Finally her eyes said she understood, and he released his grip on her mouth.

He was treading water for both of them.

They were a few yards off the port side of the boat. Sarducci and the others were standing at the stern, watching the garbage as it churned through the propellers. Dark smoke puffed from the boat's exhaust, in time to the loping cadence of the diesel engine.

The skipper was standing near the gunwale, mopping his bleeding head with his scarf. From the corner of his eye he caught sight of Indy and Alecia in the water. Indy held a finger to his lips and shook his head.

The boat moved slowly away.

Indy's legs felt like lead. He was nearing exhaustion.

The seaplane was behind them. The interior of the cockpit, between the wings, was lighted, and Indy could see the pilot checking a clipboard against the instrument panel. Everyone else was on the garbage boat. At least, Indy hoped they were.

"I've got you," Indy whispered in Alecia's ear. "We're going to swim very quietly, Princess. But I need you to help me—you've got to relax and let yourself float."

"Where are we going?" Alecia asked as she

watched the garbage boat move farther away in its lazy circle. She couldn't see the flying boat behind them.

"We've got a plane to catch," Indy said.

At sixteen thousand feet in the night sky, in the aft section of the starboard hull of the Savoia-Marchetti 55, behind a crate of spare parts, Alecia shivered in the dark.

"Jones," she said between her chattering teeth, "I'm freezing. I've got ice in my hair."

"We're probably three miles up," Indy said. "We've got to get out of these wet clothes."

"You w-w-wish," Alecia said.

"Don't worry," Indy said as cheerfully as he could. "Go on, strip out of them. It's as dark as a cave in here, so I'll have to use my imagination."

"I'll bet you have a g-g-good one."

"There's got to be a tarp or something around here to throw over you," Indy said. He felt his way around the crates and boxes until he came to the bulkhead and its row of tools. His stiff fingers knocked a wrench from its hook and he grimaced as it clanged against the deck.

"Sorry," he whispered.

His hands slid over more tools, then found a row of shelves. On the top shelf he found a bin, and his fingertips touched fabric. A pile of blankets. Next to the bin was a metal box. When he opened the lid his hands felt a candle and a box of matches.

"I'm going to strike a match," he said. "I won't look."

"I'm too cold to care," she said.

He lit the match and, through the vapor of his breath, inspected the contents of the metal box. It was a survival kit with first-aid supplies, canned food, a signal gun, and a flask of water. Next to the shelf was a locker, and in it hung a rack of clothes.

"Jackpot," Indy said.

He extinguished the match.

He tucked the coveralls and the blankets under his arm and, with the box in his hands, felt his way back to where Alecia sat behind the largest crate. Static electricity crackled down the length of the blanket as he unfolded it to drape around her shoulders, and for a moment Alecia's tattooed back was illuminated by a pale blue glow.

"Very inventive, Jones," Alecia said as she pulled the blanket around her. "I suppose you're going to lurch into me next—purely by accident, of course."

"Sure," he said. "Here, I've found some food. You can start on these. It *feels* like a box of crackers."

"I don't care if it's sparking plugs, I'll eat them."

Indy handed her the box.

"My turn to change," he said. He peeled painfully out of his clothes, then slipped into the pair of mechanic's coveralls he'd found in the locker. Then he took one of the candles from the survival kit, lit it with shaking fingers, and dribbled a few drops of wax on the deck between them.

"Is it safe?" she asked.

"I don't smell any gasoline back here," he said as he placed the candle in the wax. "Then again, my nose is full of ice. I can't smell anything."

Alecia took another blanket and began to shake the ice from her hair. "This has been a red-letter day," she said. "I've been shot at, almost blown up, and very nearly burned to death. I've been chased by some charming gentlemen in black and dumped into the sea with a load of garbage to drown. To top it off, I'm in danger of freezing to death in the belly of a fascist airplane going God knows where—and all within less than twenty-four hours of meeting you. Jones, is your life always like this?"

"No," Indy said. "Sometimes it gets exciting." He peeled the lid from one of the tins, jabbed a forefinger into it, and touched the finger to the tip of his tongue. "Sardines," he complained.

"I love sardines," Alecia said.

"Take 'em," Indy said. He picked another from the box and removed the lid. "Can you read Italian? Neither can I. They say air travel is the wave of the future. If so, they'd better improve the food. Ah, this is better."

"What is it?"

"Potted meat of some kind," he said.

As Indy ate he took his revolver and began to dry it on the blanket. When he broke it open to inspect the cartridges, a slender cylinder of ice slid from the barrel and shattered on the floor.

"My wristwatch doesn't work, either," Indy said, shaking it and then holding it to his ear. "But I'd say we've been in the air for an hour or so now. We're probably on our way to Rome."

"How long will it take?"

"Rome is what, two thousand miles from London as the crow flies? Another ten, maybe twelve hours. If we're lucky, they won't check this hold until we land."

"And if we're not lucky?"

Indy shrugged.

"It's better than drowning, Princess."

Alecia finished the last of the sardines and laid the

tin aside. She pulled the blanket tighter around her and scooted over next to Indy.

"Jones," she said.

"Yeah?"

"I want to thank you," she said. "This has been the most terrifying day of my life, but I've never felt more alive. And I know that I'm in this because of Alistair, not because of you."

Indy pretended to inspect the Webley. Alecia placed her hand over the barrel and took the gun away from him.

"Look at me," she said. "No matter what happens—whether I live through this or not—I want you to know that I don't regret a minute of it."

"God help me," Indy said, and looked into her eyes.

He kissed her. Despite the garbage and the seawater and the sardines, she still tasted wonderful. The blanket slid from her shoulders, but despite the cold she made no move to retrieve it. When their lips parted, he found himself fighting for air once more.

"Alecia," he gasped.

"Look, Jones, we could be dead in the next fifteen minutes. One of those thugs in black could walk through that hatch and it would be the end of both of us. Nobody, and I mean nobody, would ever know what happened to us. I'm trying to tell you that I—"

Indy pinched her lips shut.

"Don't say it," he pleaded. "If you say it, I have to say it, and then you're a goner for sure. I can't explain it, just trust me. You've nearly gotten rubbed out four or five times already, and that's when I thought I didn't like you."

"What in bloody hell are you talking about?" She

picked up a pair of coveralls from the pile of clothes Indy had brought and began to put them on. Indy turned his head. "If you find me unappealing, all you have to do is say so. I know I'm just a librarian, Dr. Jones—surely not as glamorous as the women you have scattered all over the world—but at least I'm sincere. You don't have to make up excuses."

"I was trying to explain," he said.

"Explain what?" She buttoned up the coveralls, wiped a tear from her cheek, and pulled the blanket tightly around her.

"That I can't allow myself to feel anything for you," he said. "When I was in the jungle a few weeks ago I came into contact with this, this *artifact*, and it carried a particularly nasty . . . warning."

"You mean a curse?"

Indy's head bobbed. It was neither a shake nor a nod, but something in between.

"Forgive me, but you're capable of better than that," Alecia said. "I would have expected you to tell me that you were married, or that your fiancée was dying of some terrible illness, or that you had a war injury. But a curse? Low marks indeed."

Indy swallowed.

"Not only don't you find me attractive, you don't trust me, either. Why is trust so difficult for you? No, don't answer, it doesn't matter. I can accept your hating me. It's best that I remind myself that I'm on this— *adventure*—to find my brother."

"Alecia," Indy said, "I just don't want anything to happen."

"You've bloody well proved that," she said. "Now, if

you don't mind, I'm going to get some rest. If I'm to be shot in a few hours, I'd like to be awake for it."

When the drone of the engines lessened in pitch, Indy snapped awake. The shafts of sunlight streaming in through the starboard portholes began to swing in unison over the interior of the cargo hold as the flying boat began a sweeping downward turn on its final approach to Ostia, the seaplane base near Rome.

Balbo's armada, Indy saw from a porthole, was already moored at the docks, like some gargantuan flock of Canada geese. The harbor was filled with ships of every description, and fireboats were shooting blasts of water in the air to celebrate the triumph.

"Alecia," Indy said. "It's time."

"No," she murmured. "Let me sleep just a little longer."

"Okay, but you'll miss your execution."

Her eyes opened.

"I thought it was all a dream," she said.

She sat up and rubbed her eyes. "My God, I'm still on this horrible flying boat. But at least it's warm again. Do you really think they'll shoot us?"

"Not unless they find us," Indy said. "Help me clean up this mess. I think we can squeeze into the lockers and hide there until it's safe to leave."

6

TOWER OF THE WINDS

Long after the motors had been silenced and the SM.55 had been safely moored, a pair of unlikely-looking mechanics exited the flying boat from the hatch at the nose of the starboard hull and walked unsteadily down the gangplank toward the dock. The taller one swung a heavy red toolbox in his right hand, while the smaller of the two—face hidden behind a floppy aviator's helmet—trailed a few steps behind. At the end of the gangway a fascist soldier leaned against his rifle, smoking a cigarette. He studied the pair coming toward him.

Indy nodded as they passed.

"Uno momento," the soldier said. He cradled the bolt-action rifle in the crook of his left arm while he fumbled in the breast pocket of his uniform for a sheet of paper. He unfolded the paper and studied it while the cigarette dangled from the corner of his mouth, his eyes squinting against the smoke.

Indy grinned.

"Mozzarella," he mumbled.

"*Che ha detto?*" the soldier asked, studying the list. He took one last drag on the cigarette and flicked the butt into the water.

Indy jerked his thumb toward Alecia.

"Ravioli."

Alecia nodded, and the movement caused a wisp of red hair to escape from her cap and droop over her right eye. The soldier stared for a moment, then dropped the list and tried to bring up the rifle.

Indy swung the heavy toolbox against the side of his head. The rifle clattered on the planks while the soldier went backward over the rail into the water.

Indy looked to see if anyone had heard the splash. They were alone at the dock. With the edge of his shoe, he nudged the rifle into the water.

They hid behind a utility shed on the dock while they stripped off the mechanic's coveralls. Their own clothes, now nearly dry, were underneath.

Indy opened the toolbox and took out his satchel. Then he struggled into his leather jacket.

"Mozzarella and Ravioli?" Alecia asked as she tossed the cap into the water and ran her hands through her hair. "That's all you could think of to call us? Not Botticelli and Raphael, or Polo and Columbo? And what's wrong with Marconi? I *like* him."

Indy placed the beaten and water-stained fedora on his head and tried to snap the brim.

"I'm still hungry," he said.

Indy and Alecia arrived in Rome following a short trip at top speed with a driver who spoke not a word of English but who kept up a nonstop monologue nonetheless, pausing only to lay upon the horn and curse the stupidity of other drivers. The wheels of the aging yellow Fiat never stopped until they pulled to the curb in front of the Inghilterra on the Via Bocca di Leone.

"I guess he assumes all speakers of English stay at the Hotel England," Alecia remarked as Indy placed some lira in the driver's outstretched hand. "I have always heard of this place, but never thought I would stay here. How delightful a bath and a change of clothes will be."

"Guess again, Princess," Indy said as he watched the Fiat speed recklessly into the night. "If he knows that all English-speaking foreigners stay here, then so do Mussolini's secret police. It's not for us."

They kept walking.

It was the day after the return of the aerial armada, but the Eternal City was still dizzy with the exploits of Balbo and his *atlantici*. Mussolini had embraced Balbo the moment he stepped ashore, planting fraternal kisses on both of the aviator's cheeks. The Atlantic, he proclaimed, had become an Italian pond. In their white dress uniforms, the cadre marched triumphantly beneath the Arch of Constantine, as if they were a returning Roman legion.

At the Royal des Étrangers near the Piazza Colonna, Indy approached the front desk while Alecia took a seat in the lobby with a cautious view of the front door.

"Do you speak English?" Indy asked.

"Absolutely!" the proprietor, a bald-headed man with a flowing mustache, exclaimed. "Grammatically! How you do. My name is Giuseppe Rinaldi."

"Look, Rinaldi," Indy said, leaning on the counter. "This establishment—is it discreet?"

"But of course," Rinaldi said. "Il Duce and his mistress once stay here, and Rinaldi tell no one. Rinaldi take secret to his grave."

"Wonderful," Indy said.

"You are lovers, no?" Rinaldi asked, then bit his knuckles. "A bit of intrigue? She belongs, perhaps, to someone else—the wife of another man!—and you have come to celebrate your forbidden love in the most beautiful city in the world? My heart break for you. But Rinaldi understand."

"No, you don't understand," Indy said. "We are not lovers."

"Ah, of course not," Rinaldi said, and winked conspiratorially.

"Separate rooms," Indy said.

"Absolutely!" Rinaldi produced a pair of brass keys. "Six American dollars."

"How much for our names not to be on the register, and our memory never to pass Rinaldi's lips?"

"Ah, that would be eight dollars American."

"Rinaldi had better be speaking truthfully as well as grammatically," Indy said. "I will pay for two nights, in advance. If no one bothers us, this rich American will leave Rinaldi a big tip when he leaves. Understand?"

"Absolutely," Rinaldi said.

Indy paid in lira. Rinaldi calculated the exchange rate—he apologetically rounded it off to the nearest thousand lira while complimenting the rich American on his choice of lodging—and pushed the keys across the counter.

"Do you think Rinaldi could come up with some

clothes to fit the rich American and the lady?" Indy
asked. "Can you have our clothes laundered while we
are taking supper this evening?"

"Absolutely. I send them up, no time at all."

Indy nodded and slipped the keys in his pocket.

"We'll leave our things outside the door," Indy said.

"There will be a small charge," Rinaldi said. "Our
restaurant is *buono*. Very good! She is just next door and
has plenty view of the piazza."

Indy turned to leave.

"Boss," Rinaldi said. Indy paused. "The rooms they
are connected. A door, you understand? Enjoy."

At the sidewalk café downstairs, Indy drank coffee
with the viscosity of motor oil and skimmed the *New
York Herald Tribune* while waiting for Alecia to finish
her bath. The Piazza Colonna was dominated by a huge
banner showing Mussolini in an aviator's costume with a
map of the flight in the background. A series of white
lightbulbs traced the journey across the Atlantic, while
red ones marked the return.

"You'd think it had been Mussolini at the stick,"
Alecia commented as she sat down next to Indy. She was
wearing a long, emerald-green evening gown that
showed more of her than Indy was comfortable with.
With his heart in his throat, he glanced away and tapped
the newspaper.

"It says here that Mussolini has appointed Balbo air
marshal—whatever that means," Indy said. "They lost
one of their planes on takeoff at Ponta Delgada; it over-
turned, killing one of the pilots."

"I'm glad I didn't know that before," Alecia said.

"Actually, they had predicted the loss of at least
four of the twenty-five planes during the flight. That's

the ratio they had experienced during previous long-distance flights. Can you imagine setting out knowing that there was one chance in six that you wouldn't make it back?"

"There's a name for that," Alecia said. "Russian roulette. These aviators are lunatics handling a loaded gun. With those odds, air travel is obviously never going to catch on. It's ships and trains for me, Jones."

"Feel better?" Indy asked. "I was getting a little worried."

"Sorry," she said. "I dozed off in the tub. I had forgotten how wonderful it feels to be clean."

"You look gorgeous," Indy blurted. Then: "I mean, Rinaldi must have a practiced eye for dress sizes."

"Actually, it's a little tight."

Indy reached absentmindedly for his coffee and trailed the sleeve of his ill-fitting pin-striped suit through the butter dish.

"Where in the world did they dig up that suit?" Alecia asked as Indy wiped at the sleeve with a table napkin. "You look like something from a gangster movie."

"Rinaldi probably gets his idea of American fashion from those movies," Indy said.

"Don't be too hard on him," Alecia said. "You Americans do seem to glorify gangsters. As mysterious as you were at the desk, he probably thought John Dillinger and his gun moll were staying with him."

"I'm sure he'll put it in the next travel guide," Indy said as he rolled up his sleeves to the elbow. "Still, there is quite a lot of room for the old gat under the arm."

"But your gat shoots icicles," Alecia said.

Indy cleared his throat.

"Sorry, Jones," Alecia said. "It's just that I think you look adorable in that stupid suit, and I hate myself for it. I'm behaving childishly, and I apologize."

"You don't understand," Indy said.

"The curse," Alecia said.

"If I didn't—feel so drawn to you—there wouldn't be a problem. I know it sounds insane, but I've seen enough of this mumbo jumbo to know that it sometimes can be a self-fulfilling prophecy. I just don't want to take the chance."

"Yeah?" Alecia asked. "Then why don't you try hating me? At least it's some kind of passion. You already said you don't trust me. It can't be that much of a jump to really despise me."

Indy looked away.

Alecia leaned close.

"Try it, Jones," she whispered. "Look me in the eyes and tell me you hate me. Tell me you've never hated anybody so much, never felt so violently out of control when they were around, that I just make you want to scream."

Indy could feel her breath on his neck.

"Say it," she murmured, and took his face in her hands. "Tell me that you hate my guts."

Their lips brushed as the waiter came.

Indy coughed and pulled at his collar. Alecia folded her arms across her chest and stared at the ceiling, silently cursing the waiter's timing.

"Back to business, then," she said when the waiter had gone. "We've made it this far. It's after ten. There obviously isn't anything we can do tonight, so we'll have to make a fresh start of it in the morning. What's your plan, Jones?"

"My plan is to find Sarducci," Indy said. "He's the key to all of this: the theft of the manuscript, the disappearance of Alistair, the attempts on you." He was afraid to bring up the Crystal Skull.

"Sarducci has to know where Alistair is," Alecia said. "He can't have been trying to kill us just for fun."

"I wouldn't go that far," Indy said. "He's capable, I think, of just about anything."

"Ironic, isn't it?" Alecia asked. "We were aboard the same plane with this maniac, terrified of being murdered at any moment, and now we're purposely going looking for him. So how do we do it?"

"That's the easy part," Indy said. "He's a curator of some sort for the Museum of Antiquity here, not to mention a fairly important member of Mussolini's secret police. We have to get him alone somehow. But the real question is, what do we do once we have him?"

Indy and Alecia walked through the bronze doors of the Museum of Antiquity as the clocks of the city were chiming nine o'clock the next morning. On each door was a boldly executed fasces, the symbol of ancient Rome: a bundle of rods strapped together around an ax, signifying the unbreakable power of the state.

Alecia wore sunglasses and had a scarf tied tightly around her head, while Indy kept his hat low over his eyes.

"You should have stayed behind," Indy told her as they walked through the lobby, pausing only long enough to pay for a guidebook. "It's too dangerous for you here."

"Nothing doing," Alecia said. "I'm not about to sit

alone in a hotel room. I'm in this to find my brother. Besides, what are they going to do to us in a museum?"

Indy didn't answer. They were walking past a working model of a guillotine used during the French Revolution, the blade stained all too realistically with the blood of intellectuals and aristocrats.

"Kind of bloodthirsty, don't you think?" Alecia asked.

"Fascism is based on violence," Indy said. "The state is supreme, and the state's avowed purpose is to wage war. Mussolini himself coined the term, his contribution to the twentieth century. Do you have the map?"

Alecia opened the guidebook.

"Here's the floor plan," she said. "My word, it's like the catacombs in here. See anything that might resemble Sarducci's office?

"Here," she said. *Maestro di archeologia.*"

"That would be it," Indy said. "This way."

They turned down a long corridor. Their footsteps rang on the marble floor. Finally they came to a heavy oak door with a brass nameplate: LEONARDO SARDUCCI.

"He might not even be here," Alecia said.

"He's in there," Indy said. "I can smell him."

"So, do we knock or what?"

Indy reached down to try the knob, but before his fingers could grasp it, the door swung inward. A dark-haired Italian girl in a white blouse and gray skirt smiled at them.

"Dottore Jones?" she asked. "Signorina Dunstin. Come in, please. The maestro has been expecting you."

"Geesh," Indy said.

"Great thinking, Jones," Alecia said.

"It's quite all right," the secretary said. "Come in.

Dottore Sarducci will be with you shortly. Would you care for something to drink? Coffee, perhaps? Or tea?"

They stepped into the anteroom. The secretary showed them to the sofa, then brought coffee and tea on a silver service. She poured for them.

"My name is Caramia," she said pleasantly. "Your stay in Rome has been good, no?"

"Very nice," Indy answered with a smile.

Alecia elbowed him in the ribs.

"Sorry," Indy said.

"Don't forget that these are the people who have been trying to kill us," she said. "For all we know, these cups are laced with cyanide."

"Oh no, it's quite safe," the secretary said. "One's office is—how do you say it in English?—sanctuary. The *dottore* says that one should never befoul one's nest with guilty blood. There is a place to act like beasts, and a place to act like men, no?"

"Your doctor is very clever," Indy said. "Insane, but clever."

"Perhaps," she said. Caramia poured herself a cup of coffee and heaped sugar into it. "But I was locked away in an asylum at sixteen years of age for disobeying my parents. I did not want to marry the man they had chosen for me because I did not love him. I felt like a prostitute. It was a business transaction—my parents had already spent the dowry. They said I would grow to love him, but that could not be true. He beat his animals and he beat me. So I ran away, and they had me locked up. Until I came to my senses, they said. Well, the *dottore* saved me. He gave me back my dignity, and for that I am eternally grateful."

"He murders people," Indy said.

Caramia shrugged.

"It is just a word," she said. "To kill for pleasure, that is murder. To kill for your country, that is heroic."

"Aren't you afraid of the police?" Alecia asked.

"The *dottore is* the police." Caramia smiled a Mona Lisa smile above her cup.

The buzzer on her desk rang.

"He will see you now." Caramia set her cup on the desk. "Before you enter," she said. "Your pistol. You may keep the whip."

Indy sighed and removed the Webley from his waistband.

Caramia examined the revolver with distaste. Veins of rust had begun to form on the finely blued steel, and she had to slap the cylinder to break it free. She shook the cartridges out into a drawer on her desk.

"You really ought to take better care of your weapons," Caramia said as she handed the revolver back to Indy. "Your life may depend upon it someday."

"Sorry," Indy said. "Haven't had time to clean it since we were dumped into the channel with a load of garbage by your boss and his goons."

Caramia made a clucking sound with her tongue.

"You should make time," she said.

Caramia went to a pair of broad double doors and swung them open. When Indy and Alecia had stepped inside, the doors swung shut. Indy heard the click of the lock.

The room was a magnificent corner office, and everything—from the rug on the floor to the books lining the shelves to the swords upon the wall—dated from the Renaissance. Sarducci sat in a swivel chair behind a massive desk with his back turned toward them, staring out over the city. The morning sun gleamed off his bald head.

Indy and Alecia walked forward and stood uncomfortably in front of the desk. Indy plucked a sword from a basket near the desk and ran his thumb along the blade.

"It's quite real," Sarducci said, his back still turned. "It was made in Toledo, some six hundred years ago. And still as lethal as the day it was made. Are you considering plunging it into my heart?"

Indy rubbed a drop of blood between his thumb and forefinger.

"I would," he said, "if I thought you had one."

Sarducci laughed and spun the chair around.

"I've missed your wit, Dr. Jones," he said. "And I'm afraid that I underestimated you during our first meeting. Why, all of the reports made you seem like a clown, some type of mad Boy Scout with a shovel. Imagine my delight when I discovered that your head was doing something more than holding up that awful-looking hat."

"I like my hat," Indy said, taking it off and looking at the stains. "Sure, it's a little beat-up, but when it's blocked it will be as good as new."

"The eternal optimist," Sarducci said. "It was really quite clever how you saved yourselves by sneaking aboard the aircraft. I never suspected until, of course, we discovered the soldier you had knocked senseless."

"He's okay?" Indy asked as he replaced his hat.

"Alas, I'm afraid not," Sarducci said. "After we pulled him from the water, I was forced to have him shot for being such a half-wit."

Indy closed his eyes.

"Don't you have chairs for your guests?" Alecia asked.

"I prefer them to stand," Sarducci said. "The psychology of power, you know."

"Of course."

"Forgive me, but we haven't been formally introduced. How rude of me, when Dr. Jones and I have been chatting like old school chums. I am Leonardo Sarducci; and you, I presume, are Miss Alecia Dunstin."

"You know bloody well who I am," Alecia said. "Where's Alistair?"

"Patience, patience," Sarducci pleaded. "First things first. It is a pleasure to make your acquaintance, Miss Dunstin. Please, remove your scarf and glasses so that I can take a better look at you. I never got the chance during our little game."

"No," Alecia said. "Why don't you unlock the door?"

"You can't expect me to let you walk out of here, just like that?" Sarducci asked. "No, the door will remain locked until we talk this over and come to some kind of . . . resolution. Didn't Caramia explain the rules to you?"

"She said you wouldn't hurt us," Alecia said.

"Oh, I won't—not here." Sarducci stood and walked around the end of the desk.

"I knew you would come," he said. "You couldn't stay away. The link was too obvious for you to resist, when a superior mind could have conjured up a thousand other solutions. But not you, my American cowboy."

"I've always liked westerns," Indy said.

"But I'm glad you're here. You have proved to be a

most capable opponent, a challenge of the sort that I've never encountered before. It would be a shame to waste all of that cunning. Since you're going to lose in the end, why don't you admit defeat and join me?"

"You read too much Machiavelli."

"Ah, but the master was right. You should always offer your most capable opponents the opportunity to join you. And if they refuse, crush them."

Sarducci stood in front of Alecia for a moment, then reached a black-gloved hand toward her face.

Indy grabbed his wrist.

"Don't touch her," he said through clenched teeth.

"Does she mean something to you?" Sarducci asked with Indy's hand still clamped around his wrist. "Do you feel something tender for her, Dr. Jones?"

"No," Indy said, letting go.

"Ah, you mustn't forget the curse," Sarducci taunted. "How good it was of you to touch the Crystal Skull with your bare fingers and remove it from its alcove, to bear the brunt of all those centuries for my sake. Amazing, is it not, how well it has all worked out."

"Still believing in fairy tales, eh?"

"Come now, Dr. Jones," Sarducci said. "Fairy tales indeed. Poor Miss Dunstin was never in danger until you showed up, acting the swashbuckler. How many times have you managed to save her so far? How long do you think you can keep it up? As soon as you walk out of that door—assuming that you do—it will all start over again. You'll forever be watching over your shoulder, forever apprehensive of every sound in the night, until the inevitable moment when your attention lags and you make one small mistake."

"Stop it," Alecia said.

Sarducci laughed.

"I do hope you haven't made love to her," he said. "That would seal her fate, wouldn't it? To consummate your love would be to court certain disaster. Perhaps you've only managed to get her this far because you have resisted, fought the attraction, denied your feelings. But for how long? You will let your guard down sooner or later, Dr. Jones, perhaps tonight, under the influence of our beautiful full moon. You will offer yourself handy rationalizations about myths and superstitions, and then you will lose what you love most in the world."

"Go to hell," Indy said.

"Of course I will," Sarducci said. "But not for a very, very long time yet. Like Faust, I have made my deal and am merely biding my time until the devil pays in full. But you, my friend, are already there." He chuckled.

"However, there is a way out," he said. "Join me and you can extinguish all the love in your heart. Love is such a pitiful human emotion! It encourages us to be weak, to make sacrifices, to place the welfare of others before ourselves. How contrary to the rules of survival. Miss Dunstin's brother has seen the truth in what I say, although reluctantly at first, and now the world awaits him. Take the dark path, Dr. Jones. Then you can have your fill of her and never once look back."

"You're sick," Indy said. "I mean, literally sick. I feel sorry for you, Leonardo, because I know that you were once capable of love. Can't you understand that you're ill, that it was the head wound—"

"Stop," Sarducci said, grimacing in pain. He put a hand to his forehead. "It is well documented that the manifestation of genius is often preceded by violent trauma." He breathed deeply and smiled. "Now, if you please," he told Alecia.

"You are insane," she said. She removed the glasses and pulled the scarf from her hair. "There. Are you pleased? Are you imagining how I'll look when I'm dead, dead, dead! Now tell me where my brother is."

Sarducci stood for a moment with a look of recognition, then utter shock. He put a hand to his mouth and stumbled backward, leaning against the edge of his desk for support.

"Mona," he gasped.

Alecia looked questioningly at Indy.

"Mona," Sarducci said again.

Indy took Alecia by the arm and guided her toward the door.

"We don't know where Alistair is," she protested.

"Yes, we do. He's with them. That's all we need to know," Indy said. "Ask him to unlock the door."

Sarducci seemed to be recovering.

"I will set you free," he said unsteadily. "For my Mona. But as soon as you cross that threshold, it begins anew. Miss Dunstin, we will meet again. But sadly, Dr. Jones, I cannot say the same of you. As your poet said, you are as one whose name is written upon the water. Farewell." Sarducci paused.

"One last thing," he said, "so that you don't leave empty-handed. I know how even the smallest morsel of hope can sustain those who are desperate, so I give it to you not out of compassion but in hopes of prolonging your agony: Alistair is beneath the red sun." Sarducci pushed the intercom.

"Caramia," he said. "Unlock the door."

. . .

Indy pulled Alecia through the anteroom and into the corridor, their feet sliding on the marble.

"Good-bye," Caramia called.

"That was a brilliant plan, Jones," Alecia fumed. "It worked really well. It had everything—the element of surprise, superior numbers, unbridled stupidity. *What were you thinking?*"

They raced into the main hall, past the model of the guillotine, and were almost in the lobby when the phone at the desk rang. The guard picked it up.

"Not that way," Indy said, and pulled her down another corridor. Their footsteps sounded like thunder slapping against the floor.

"Take your shoes off," he said.

"What?"

"Kick 'em off."

They continued in stocking feet down another passage, then up a flight of stairs, and at an exhibit on ancient Rome, Indy relieved a wax figure of a Roman legionnaire of his sword.

"Do you know how to use that thing?"

"Theoretically," Indy said.

"How well do you dance?" Alecia asked.

"What's that got to do with it?"

"An old Celtic proverb says, Never give a sword to a man who can't dance," Alecia said. "Well, can you dance?"

"You can't swim," he said. "Everybody has *something* they can't do."

"Give me the sword," she said.

A guard appeared at the end of the hallway, block-

ing their path. They slid for several feet on the slick
marble floor before they could reverse their motion.

"Fermata!" the guard cried. He carried a short-bar-
reled automatic rifle with a large ammunition clip.

"They're awfully fond of machine guns around
here," Indy said as they raced around a corner. Alecia
grabbed his collar and pulled him against the wall.

She put a finger to her lips.

The sound of the guard's shoes thundered toward
them. Alecia held the sword poised over her right shoulder. When the barrel of the gun popped around the
corner, Alecia sliced downward with the sword. Sparks
flew as the heavy blade knocked the rifle to the floor.

The stunned guard stood flat-footed in front of her,
and Alecia brought the sword back around and smacked
him on the forehead with the broad side of the blade.
He sprawled unconscious on the floor.

Indy snatched up the gun.

"I suppose you want this, too?" he asked.

"I don't like guns," Alecia said.

They went back around the corner, stepping over
the guard, and into another hall. The large room was
dedicated to the civilizations of Central and South
America. Alecia tugged on Indy's sleeve and pointed at a
row of windows that lined the other side of the room.
Beyond the windows, Indy could see the stone balustrade of a balcony overlooking the street.

They could hear shouting on the floor below them.
They ran past the glass cases containing collections of
Aztec, Mayan, and Incan artifacts. "Not bad," Indy exclaimed as they passed beneath a reconstructed stone
arch that had been excavated at Tulúm.

Suddenly Indy slid to a stop in his stocking feet.

"What's wrong?" Alecia shouted. "Let's go."

Sitting atop a stone pedestal, enclosed in a cube of thick glass, was the Crystal Skull. Illuminated by a lamp placed in the base, the eye sockets glowed with an unearthly light.

Alecia stood beside Indy.

"That's it, isn't it?" she asked.

Indy clawed at the glass, then tried to tip the pedestal over. It wouldn't budge. He struck the glass with the butt of the gun, but he couldn't make so much as a crack in it.

"Jones, they're coming," Alecia said.

"But I've got to have it," he said. "It's our chance."

"There's no time," Alecia said.

Indy backed away from the case, snapped off the safety on the machine gun, and aimed for the top of the case. He was counting on luck to keep him from destroying the skull as well.

"Stand back," he warned.

Alecia ducked behind a column. Indy pulled the trigger and the staccato of the machine-gun burst was deafening in the hall, followed by the sharp whine of ricochets as the slugs bounced off the glass.

The skull rocked slightly on its base, and the movement made the finely articulated jaw click open and shut, open and shut, as if it were laughing at Indy.

"It's bulletproof!" Indy screamed.

"They certainly know where we are now," Alecia said.

"Sarducci did this on purpose," Indy fumed. "He knew this would happen. He's teasing me. I hate you! Do you hear me, Sarducci, you bald sack of—"

His words were drowned amid the shattering of

glass. Alecia had tossed the sword through one of the windows. Then she grabbed Indy's sleeve and pulled him away from the Crystal Skull. Indy snatched the identification tag from the display case as he went by, and stuffed it into his pocket.

A pair of guards burst through the door on the opposite side of the room, and Indy fired a long burst into the ceiling over their heads. As plaster and bits of wood rained down they ducked back outside the doorway.

"Come on," Alecia said as she stepped through the frame of the broken window. Indy followed, and they ran to the balustrade and peered over.

They were forty feet above the sidewalk. Below them was the museum's sidewalk café, and at the curb was parked a farm truck delivering the day's supplies.

"We've got to jump," Indy said.

"Are you crazy?"

A bullet chipped the stone handrail.

"Forget it," she said. "Of course you are."

Indy tossed the gun aside. Alecia clutched his hand as they vaulted over.

They landed on the cartons of vegetables stacked in the back of the farm truck. "They use a lot of tomatoes," Indy said, inspecting the stains on his trousers. They scrambled down and hid behind the side of the truck while the guards looked over the stone railing. The men who had been unloading the produce began to shout and point to the other side of the truck.

"Great," Indy said. "They'll be down here in a minute. And I threw away the only gun I had that works. You don't even have your sword."

An aging black limousine pulled to a careful stop

beside the truck. The driver got calmly out, opened the rear door, and motioned for them to get inside.

"What in the world?" Indy exclaimed.

"We're not in a position to ask," Alecia said as she pulled Indy toward the open door. "When are you going to stop looking a gift horse in the mouth?"

They climbed into the limousine and the driver shut the door behind them. Then he returned to the wheel, carefully signaled, and pulled smoothly into the street.

Behind them, the guards were spilling onto the sidewalk.

"I was this close to getting the skull," Indy told Alecia, holding his thumb and forefinger a fraction of an inch apart. "This close. If you'd just given me a little more time, I would have figured it out."

"Jones," Alecia said. "Aren't you going to thank our saviors?"

"Thanks," Indy told the old couple that were sitting in the seat across from them. "But I was this close," he said. "Why'd you stop to help us, anyway?"

"We're always ready to help those in need," the old man said with a French accent, and shrugged as if it were nothing. "You two looked as if you were in need."

The couple both had hair of the purest white, and clear blue eyes. They wore old-fashioned clothes of the kind that had been popular a century ago. The old man rested his hands upon a cane that was between his knees, and the woman kept her hands folded peacefully in her lap.

"Sorry about your seat," Indy apologized, indicating the tomato stains.

"Not to worry," the woman said. "Sebastian can get

it out, I'm sure. He's handled more difficult problems than that in the past."

"Sebastian?" Indy asked. "That's your husband?"

"Oh no, that's our driver," the man said. "Although he's really more of a son to us than a servant. I am Nicholas and this is Perenelle. Oh, no need to introduce yourself. We know who you are."

Indy brightened.

"You've heard of me, then."

"Followed you very closely, as a matter of fact," the old man remarked with a twinkle in his eye. "We couldn't help but stop when we spotted you on the street. And this charming young woman, Dr. Jones. She must be your fiancée, because I don't recall having read that you are married."

Alecia introduced herself.

"We aren't engaged," she said. "We've only known each other for a couple of days, but it does seem like years. I guess you would have to describe us as friends."

"That's good," the old woman said. "The world needs more friends, don't you think? Remain friends, and the rest will take care of itself."

"Yes," Alecia said. "I suppose so."

"Your work interests me a great deal, you know," the old man told Indy. "The more we learn about the past, the more we learn about ourselves. There's really nothing new under the sun. It's all been done before, at one time or another. Don't you agree?"

"To some extent," Indy said cautiously.

"To every extent," the man said flatly. "Empires crumble, cities fall. Youth fades and passes away. But the human soul remains the same. The important thing is not the destination, but the journey. Wealth is only worthwhile if you put it to use for the good of others. As the Bible says, what does it profit a man to gain the whole world only to lose his own soul?"

Indy dared a glance at Alecia.

"The world is on the brink of a terrible power it does not understand," the old man said suddenly, his blue eyes blazing. He seemed to grow younger as he spoke. "God made us just a little lower than the angels, put a little spark of the divine in each of us, but with that power comes responsibility. We are free to choose. We can make this world a paradise, or turn it into a hell upon earth."

"Sir," Indy asked, "what exactly are you speaking of?"

"Nothing," the old man said. "Everything. With each decision we make, the scales tip a little more in one direction or the other."

"Nicholas," the woman cautioned.

"I'm sorry," he said, and he seemed ancient once more. "I don't mean to bother you with the talk of a foolish old man."

"It's no bother," Indy said.

Suddenly the old man reached out and gave Indy's knee a fatherly pat. "I know you're doing your best," he said. "Just keep your feet upon the path, son, and you'll be fine. The most precious commodity in the world is not gold, or power, or fame. It's love. Isn't it, dear?"

The limousine stopped.

"Here we are," the woman announced.

"Where?" Alecia asked.

"Why, the Vatican, of course," the old woman said. "You did say you wanted to visit your friend from America, didn't you? This is where he spends most of his time, poring over all those dusty records. Tell him for us that he needs to get out more, won't you?"

"Of course," Indy said.

Sebastian opened the door.

"Good-bye," the old man said. "And Godspeed."

"I'd find some shoes if I were you," the old woman advised. "You're likely to catch your death of cold running around in your stockings."

In a moment the limousine had pulled away.

Indy and Alecia passed through the Gate of St. Anne into the Vatican City and down the curving road to the Court of Belvedere. At the foot of the stairway leading to the Vatican Library, beside the statue of the third-century antipope Hippolytus, a blue-and-yellow-uniformed Swiss guard asked their business.

"We're here to see Professor Morey," Indy said. "I'm a colleague from Princeton University."

"He is in the Secret Archives," the guard replied in perfect English. "It is in the Tower of the Winds. But you need permission from the prefect."

"No," Alecia said. She brushed her hair from her eyes and stared at him intently. "We do not have a pass. But certainly if Dr. Morey has been granted such permission, it would be appropriate for us to visit him there."

The guard blinked, as if he had lost his train of thought.

"The Tower of the Winds," he repeated.

"Yes, thank you," Alecia said.

She and Indy ascended the stairs, leaving the guard standing at the base.

"How do you do that?" Indy asked.

"Do what?" she inquired innocently. Then: "Why do they call it the Secret Archives if they actually give passes for people to dig around there?"

"They were secret for centuries," Indy said. "They contain the personal archives of the popes and they weren't opened to scholars until 1881. They are still off-limits to journalists and photographers."

"How much material is there?"

"Nobody knows for sure," Indy said. "It isn't indexed in any reasonable fashion. Placed end to end, there are seven and a half miles of shelves filled with tons of material. Morey has been working to document all of the Vatican's early Christian art collection for years."

After passing another Swiss guard who seemed to be momentarily confused about his duty, they found Charles Rufus Morey in the Meridian Room, beneath a huge painting of the storm in the Sea of Galilee. His glasses were propped on his head and he was attempting to lift a heavy leather-bound volume from a top shelf.

"Let me help you," Indy said. He took the book and wrestled it to the table.

"Thank you, Jones. Jones!" Morey exclaimed. His glasses slipped down on his nose and he glanced at his watch. "What are you doing here? You have a class to teach in an hour, you know. You'll never get back in time."

"Don't worry, sir," Indy said. "It's a long story, but my classes are being taken care of. This is Alecia Dunstin. We're doing some rather urgent—well, *research*—and we've come to ask your help."

"Help? What kind of help do you need?"

Indy pulled up a stool and sat down next to Morey. "How familiar are you with Voynich?" he asked.

Two hours later Charles Rufus Morey withdrew a handkerchief from his pocket and cleaned his glasses. "A particularly difficult problem, indeed," he said. "And not one of purely academic consequences. Tell me, Jones, have you been running around getting shot at and so forth the whole time you've been at Princeton?"

"No, sir."

"I should hope not. Now, let me see if I can help you. It will do no good to visit the Villa Mondragone at Frascati, where the manuscript was found, because all the archives there have been packed up and removed. Besides, it seems as if it found its way there as something of a curiosity. I may be biased, because my bailiwick is art history, but it seems that the colors in the manuscript are the key. Don't look for your answer in a book; look for it in art."

"What do you mean?"

"In the old days it was very common for secret information to be contained, for example, in paintings or book illustrations or even the stained glass of cathedrals —hidden and yet in plain sight, as it were. Look here." Morey searched among the books on the desk, found the right one, and opened it to the first page. It was an illustrated manuscript from the twelfth century.

"Notice the intricate borders and so forth," he said. "Not only are they pretty, but to the practiced eye they can contain a wealth of information. I'm just beginning to understand them myself."

"What do I look for, then?"

"How should I know?" Morey asked. "But the colors you mentioned as accompanying the manuscript—black, red, green, and gold—are also the colors of the alchemical progression. Look for something in which those colors dominate."

Indy put his fingers to his lips, as if he were trying to remember something important. He almost had it when Alecia called to him.

"What's that?" she asked.

Alecia was pointing upward. On the ceiling was an arrow that looked much like the needle of a compass.

"That, my dear, is an anemoscope," Morey said. "It is why they call this the Tower of the Winds. The pointer is attached to a wind vane outside, and it moves as the winds move. It was built by Pope Gregory XIII in the sixteenth century, as part of an astronomical observatory to help work out the details of a new calendar. The Council of Trent, you see, had concluded that something was wrong with the old calendar, because the vernal equinox kept occurring earlier and earlier in the year."

Morey walked over to the painting of the storm on the wall.

"Look here," he said. "There is an opening in the mouth of the figure of the south wind. Sunlight would come streaming through here, and at different seasons, a Jesuit priest would mark where the beam fell on the floor. In this way they determined the true length of the year to within one day every three thousand years. It's still the basis for the calendar we use today—the Gregorian calendar."

As Indy stood looking at the painting of the storm over the sea, and the opening where the rays of the sun had shot through and mapped time in a marriage of the symbolic and the literal, something fell into place.

"Professor," he asked. "Where does the red sun shine?"

"Why, over the Red Sea," Morey said.

"Right," Indy said. "And where along the Red Sea do you find Italian soil?"

"Libya," Alecia said.

7

SAND

As the silvered crescent of the dying moon darted between storm clouds, the outline of the *Ayesha Maru* could faintly be seen anchored just beyond the treacherous rocks that guarded the desolate coast of northeastern Libya.

Two longboats carefully threaded their way through the gauntlet of rocks, and as they neared the shore their oars were shipped and the men in their prows jumped into the waist-deep water. They guided the fragile wooden boats the remaining few yards until their keels kissed the sand of the beach.

"Well done," the hired skipper, Mordecai Marlow, told his crew. "The seven mad gods of the sea have smiled upon us this night. Quickly now, get those crates well up onto the beach before we lose the clouds and the stinking fascists spot us."

Indiana Jones hopped into the water and turned to help Alecia Dunstin over the gunwale.

"Should I take my shoes off?" she asked.

"No," Indy said. "This beach is strewn with rocks that would cut your feet to ribbons. Gather your skirt and I'll carry you. That is, if you don't mind."

"I can make it," Alecia said, and dropped into the water with her shoes in her hand. The sea came in behind her and the bottom of her skirt bloomed in the water around her as she walked onto the beach.

"See?" she said as she stood on one foot and replaced one shoe, then another. "I know just where to step."

"I hope you're always that lucky," Indy said.

The men from the *Ayesha Maru* carried the five long crates high and placed them in a row upon the beach. Their shadowy forms resembled coffins in the darkness, Indy thought.

"Well," he asked, "where are they?"

"They are here," Marlow said. "They are watching, making sure that it is not a trap. Stand still and keep your hands where they can see them."

"How many times have you done this?" Indy asked.

"In this business," Marlow said, "one doesn't count."

There came a high-pitched whistle, and at the crest of the next dune, a line of forty mounted riders appeared. They swept down upon the beach like a desert storm, silent except for the creak of leather and the dull thud of hooves in the sand. They dismounted, letting the reins of their horses droop in the sand, and with knives they quickly removed the lids from the crates. Their leader, a tall white-robed figure cradling a musket that was even taller than he was, strode from crate to crate, inspecting the contents. He handed his flintlock rifle to a lieutenant and, from the last crate, snatched up an American-made Thompson submachine gun.

"Your Highness," Marlow offered. "Let me instruct you."

The prince shrugged him away and retrieved a drum magazine from the crate. He expertly fitted the magazine to the Thompson and pulled back the bolt on top of the gun, opening the breech. A shining .45-caliber cartridge clicked upward into the receiver. He released the bolt, chambering the cartridge, and pulled the trigger.

The gun sprayed bullets and flame into the night.

Marlow squinted, afraid to look.

The prince held the Thompson over his head in triumph while the rest of the band surged forward amid cries and prayers of thanks to Allah, abandoning their ancient weapons for the modern American ones.

The prince slung the Thompson over his shoulder, retrieved the flintlock, and strode over to Marlow. He presented the ornately carved rifle to the captain.

"For you," he said. "It has been in my family since my father's grandfather. Now it is yours. Keep it well and feed it only Roman pigs."

"Thank you," Marlow said. "I will place it above my bunk in my cabin, always within reach. Prince Farqhuar, I would like you to meet Indiana Jones. He has come to fight the fascists."

Indy's eyes widened.

"An American?" the prince asked enthusiastically. "I have read of you Americans. The author Jules Verne has said that your people make the best guns in the world. He has told of how you fashioned an enormous cannon and shot three men inside a shell to the surface of the moon. Tell me, have you met this Frenchman who writes such wonderful books?"

"I am afraid not, Your Highness," Indy said. "Monsieur Verne died some years ago. And I am afraid that he was exaggerating somewhat about the moon."

The prince clutched his heart.

"What a loss!" he lamented. "I would have loved to show him my people. And the great Jules Verne lie? Never! All things are true in time. How I have longed to have a cannon such as he described, to blast the Romans back across the Mediterranean."

"It is a pretty thought," Indy agreed.

"And you, my captain," the prince asked. "To what country do you belong?"

"Ah," Marlow said, "I am a servant of all free peoples and the subject of none. A pirate for those whose causes need just a little help. But I am pleased to be of service to you, my prince, leader of the greatest people in the world."

The prince grinned knowingly and withdrew a heavy sack from beneath his robes. "As long as the price is right, eh?" he asked, and pitched the bag at Marlow's feet.

Marlow put his fingers to his mouth and whistled.

"Pull out," he called. "We've got what we came for."

"Come with us and fight the Romans," the prince urged Indy. "It is a desperate struggle, but providence is on our side. There is no greater honor than to die for the glory of Allah."

"I fight alone," Indy said.

"Pity," the prince said. "I was looking forward to many wonderful nights discussing your American storytellers. The great Mark Twain—" The prince raised his hands. "Ah, do not tell me he is gone, too. My poor heart could not bear it."

The prince mounted his horse, and the nomads disappeared as quickly and as quietly as they had appeared.

Marlow slung the gold over his shoulder and turned to Indy.

"Good-bye, Dr. Jones," he said. "I hope that you find what you are looking for. You have your compass and your map? The fascist camp is ten kilometers along the coast, toward the rising sun. May whatever God you kneel to have mercy."

"Thank you," Indy said, and shook his hand. He turned to Alecia. "This is your last chance," he said. "Marlow will take you to Cairo, and you can wait there with my friend Sallah. It would be best."

"It would," Marlow agreed. "Besides, my company can be quite entertaining, and I have plenty of money to spend when we get to Cairo. It would be a delightful interlude for a weary freedom fighter."

"Not a chance," Alecia said. "On either count."

The longboats had sprouted oars. Marlow hurried and jumped into the bow of the nearest one.

"Farewell," he called. "Take care of the redheaded one. Tame her before she tames you!"

Alecia folded her arms.

"Who does that pirate think he is?" She sniffed. "Tame me, indeed."

Indy shouldered his haversack and handed Alecia a canteen.

"Not a chance," he said, and began walking east.

"I still think we needed a couple of those guns," she said, trailing behind him.

"I thought you didn't like guns."

"I don't," she said. "I'm beginning to get a healthy respect for artillery, you know? The fascists will all have guns—big guns—and God knows what else."

"Maybe you and the prince could get together," Indy suggested. "Compare calibers, that sort of thing. Dream about cannons big enough to shoot a hole in the moon."

"Jones, you are insufferable," Alecia said. "I was just thinking of evening the odds a bit, that's all. If we have to go in there fighting to get Alistair out, I'm willing to do it."

"We're not going to get him out—that is, if he wants to come out at all—unless we pick our fight carefully," Indy said. "Mussolini has thrown everything he has into conquering Libya, and they finally won. If we're going to succeed, we're going to have to use our heads, not our trigger fingers."

Indy lay prone at the crest of a small dune, studying the fascist camp through a pair of field glasses. The camp was arranged around a protected bay, where a pair of twin-hulled flying boats rested at anchor.

"It's right where Marlow said it would be."

"How do you think he knew?" Alecia asked.

Indy grinned.

"Oh, of course," she said. "He's a pirate. He sells to both sides. But why would the Italians need American guns? Don't they have enough of their own?"

"This is an elite camp," Indy said. "Balbo uses it as a base to train his *atlantici*. The officers are allowed to choose their own weapons, and I'll bet they have the best of everything."

"What time is it?" Alecia asked.

Indy passed the binoculars to Alecia and glanced at the stars.

"Three o'clock, I'd say. Maybe three-thirty."

"It looks rather quiet down there," Alecia said.

"It's almost too dark to see anything," Indy commented. The moon was nearing the western horizon. "But there's barbed wire ringing the perimeter, with a guard tower at each corner. The big tent is probably the mess, and those half-dozen smaller ones could be the officers' quarters. The enlisted men are scattered about in the pup tents in that block to the south."

"How about Sarducci and Balbo?"

"The buildings, I'd guess, near the flagpole. It looks like this was a fishing village of some kind before the war."

"Well, it doesn't look like there are any fishermen there now," Alecia said, and put down the glasses. She rested her chin on her hands.

"Where do you think they're keeping Alistair? In a guardhouse somewhere. Maybe one of the brick buildings."

"With a compound like that," Indy said, "even if he's there against his will, they wouldn't have to lock him up. Even if he did manage to escape, where would he go? Nothing but the sea, miles of rugged coast, and inland, an ocean of sand."

"So how are we going to get away?"

"Haven't figured that one out yet," Indy said. "But it's on my list, just as soon as I find a way to get inside."

"That's comforting," Alecia said.

Indy turned over on his back and put his hat over his eyes. "The moon will be down in half an hour. That should help us get through the concertina wire, at least."

"And then?"

"I don't know," Indy said beneath the hat. "Maybe by then I'll have thought of something."

"It worries me when you start thinking," Alecia said. "You think too hard. Sort of tempting fate, in a way. Like wishing. When I was a little girl I never wished for anything too hard because I was afraid I'd jinx things. As long as I didn't think about it, then I couldn't be disappointed. Keeps life on an even keel." She looked over at Indy. "Jones?" she asked.

She picked up the glasses and again studied the camp. Not a thing was moving. Even the dogs that had been trotting on the other side of the wire seemed to have given it up for the night.

"How can you sleep at a time like this?" she asked. "You must not have a nerve in your body. I feel like a spring that's about to snap." She put the glasses down.

"Alistair was just the opposite," she said. "He always wished for things. Would scream and pout and hold his breath if he didn't get them. It was as if he did all the wishing for the both of us. Worked sometimes, too. And now I feel like half of me is gone." Alecia propped her head on her elbows.

"I've always liked this time of night," she said. "I used to stay up all night long when I was a little girl, just because I knew that everyone else was asleep and wouldn't bother me. Except for Alistair, of course. He used to wake up about this time every night and stumble to the water closet, and leave the bloody door open because he didn't know I was up. Couldn't stand it. I would cover my ears until he was finished, counting the seconds until he'd snap out the light and stumble back to bed."

Alecia turned on her side and watched Indy as he slept.

"I kind of like you like this," she said. "You're rather handsome, you know that, Jones? Kind of short on conversation at the moment, but at least you don't talk back."

"What do you think is the least guarded area in the entire camp?" Indy asked.

"You're awake."

"Hard to sleep when somebody is yakking beside you," Indy said. "But really, if you were a guard, what area would you try to avoid? You know, someplace you'd want to hurry around as quickly as possible, someplace that you'd never thought was of interest to the enemy at all? Maybe someplace where the dogs don't work as well as other places."

"The latrine," Alecia said.

"Yep," Indy said. "Does Alistair still wake up about this time of night to use the can?"

"He might," Alecia said. "I really don't know. It's been a long time since I stayed up all night—at least until I met you—and our rooms are different now than when we were kids. I don't think I'd notice if he did."

Alecia looked one last time through the glasses.

"But it's worth a try," she said. "I mean, we can't go knocking on every door in the middle of the night to find him. If we let him, maybe he'll come to us."

"Alecia," Indy said. "You're not going down there."

"Why not?"

"This is a one-man job," he said.

"Maybe it's a one-woman job, then," she said.

"I'm afraid there are no swords down there," he said. He placed his field notebook in a pocket sewn into the lining of his leather jacket. "It makes sense for me to go. Don't fight me on this, or I'll turn around and leave right now."

Alecia was silent.

"I'll take that for a yes," Indy said as he zipped up his leather jacket. He took off his fedora and looked at the brim. Then he placed it on her head.

"Keep this for me," he said. "I'll be back for it. If I'm not back by dawn—or the minute you hear shooting —get out of here as quickly as you can. Don't stick around, because you won't be able to help Alistair or I if they catch you."

"Alistair or *me*," Alecia idly corrected.

"There's enough food and water in the pack for three days. I'm leaving you the Webley—Marlow cleaned it—and a box of shells. They don't treat women terribly well in this part of the world, so don't be afraid to use it. Your best bet would be to follow the coastline back to the west. When you get back to civilization, contact Marcus Brody at the American Museum of Natural History. Agreed?"

Alecia nodded.

"Dawn," he said. He paused. "What does Alistair look like?"

"Imagine me as a man," she said. "With a short beard."

Indy stuck the wire cutters from the pack in his back pocket and set off down the ridge. Alecia watched his progress through the binoculars. He crouched low as he walked, keeping behind the dunes and rock outcroppings, and circled toward the other side of the camp.

Alecia lost sight of him.

Indy crawled the last hundred yards to the barbed wire on his knees and elbows, keeping a careful eye on the guard towers at each corner of the camp. At the first set of wires, he made sure the dogs were out of sight, then cut the bottom strands and elbowed his way into it. A barb caught his face below the right cheekbone and left a long cut. Indy winced and daubed at the blood with his sleeve, then continued across the dog run to the second set of wire. He worked the jaws of the cutters three times, and then he was into the camp itself, although he was hidden from view by the wooden latrine buildings.

"Stinks," Indy muttered. He held his breath as he slid around the side of the latrine to the front, then darted for the door. It smelled even worse inside the latrine than it did outside. The interior was lit by the dim glow of a trio of evenly spaced bulbs hanging from a frayed electrical cord. A wooden bench ran the length of the rear wall, with space for twelve men.

"Not much for privacy," Indy said.

There were funnels along the end walls, and in the center was a wash station that was gravity-fed by a tank of water resting on the ceiling joists.

Indy unsnaked his whip and flicked it around the center joist, then pulled himself up into the rafters. After returning the whip to his belt, he walked carefully to the end of the rafter until he reached the cord from which one of the bulbs hung. He reeled the cord up and, licking his fingers to protect them from the heat, unscrewed the bulb until it flickered and went out. Then he re-

peated the process with the center bulb, but not before
he got a nasty shock from the threadbare cord.

A single bulb at the far end now lit the latrine.

Indy sat down on the rafter, leaned his back against
a post, and waited. Twenty minutes later the door swung
open and he readied himself. In the poor light the
sleepy man walked into the washstand in the center of
the latrine, bumped his shin, and began cursing in Italian.

Indy relaxed.

The latrine had two other patrons during the next
thirty minutes, but neither of them had red hair. Finally,
as the sky that shone between the cracks in the roof
began to lighten and Indy prepared to leave, the door
swung open once more.

A bearded redhead in a white undershirt and khaki
shorts walked in and stopped short, regarding the lack of
illumination inside. Indy knew at once that this was Alistair.

"You'd think if Mussolini can make the trains run
on time," he said with an English accent, "they could
change a few lamps around here. What a disgrace. It's
worse than holiday camp."

He walked to one of the funnels at the lighted end
and unzipped his pants, staring idly at the wall as he did
so. Indy crept along the rafter until he was near the wall,
then eased himself down until he hung by his arms.
Then he dropped to the ground.

Startled, the man turned to see what was behind.

"Dash it all," he said. "Look what you've made me
do."

"You're consistent," Indy said. "But at least you
close the door behind you now."

"Who are you?" Alistair asked. "My God, you're an American. What are you doing here?"

Indy shushed him.

"Your sister is outside the fence waiting for you," he said. "You had better *want* to go, because if you don't, I'm going to drag you out."

"Alecia's here?"

"Are you coming or not?"

"Of course I am," he said. "Why wouldn't I? I've been waiting for days for somebody to rescue me. But who are you and how did you get in here?"

"No time to explain," Indy said.

Alistair went to the washstand and rubbed his hands under the faucet.

"Stop that," Indy said. Outside, he could hear the sounds of the camp as the men prepared for the day: engines being started, voices calling to each other, the dogs whining in their pens as they waited to be fed. "Let's go. We've only got a few minutes until it's light."

Alistair dried his hands on a towel. Indy gripped him by the back of his undershirt and hauled him toward the door.

"We're going to walk out of here like we know what we're doing," Indy told him. "We're going to stroll very casually to the rear of this latrine. Then we're going to flop on our bellies and, provided there are no dogs to greet us, crawl through a hole in the wire just as quickly as we can. And if you call out or try to run, I'm going to make certain I break your neck before they catch me. Got it?"

"Don't be silly," Alistair said.

Indy peered at the back of his neck.

"What are you looking for?"

"Nothing," Indy said. "Go."

Alistair opened the latrine door just as a soldier was reaching for the handle. Indy ducked back into the darkness as Alistair swung the door open.

"*Grazie*," the soldier said absently. As he bent over the washstand Indy and Alistair slipped outside. The sun was not yet above the horizon, but it was already light enough to see the outlines of the buildings clearly.

"We'll never get out this way," Alistair whispered. "It's too bright already. The guards in the towers will see us and cut us to ribbons."

"Keep moving," Indy said with a smile. "Maybe they've been celebrating and are sleeping it off."

"The *atlantici*?" Alistair asked.

They made it to the back of the latrine, and Indy pushed Alistair through the wire ahead of him. Then he dropped to his stomach and followed.

Across the dog run, at the outer fence, Alistair paused.

"You'd better go first," he said. "I assume you marked some kind of trail through the mines."

"Mines?"

"The entire perimeter is a minefield," Alistair said. "You didn't know that?"

Indy shrugged.

"Well, then. Can you spot the path you took to get in—depressions in the sand where your knees and elbows dug in, perhaps."

"No," Indy said. "It all looks the same from here."

"Bloody good show," Alistair said. "Do you have a knife?"

Indy took the knife from his belt and passed it hilt first.

"We'll just have to make the best of it. I knew I would probably blow myself up eventually, but I always thought it would be in my laboratory."

"Your shirt," Indy said. "Take it off and stuff it in your pocket. It's too white."

Alistair advanced cautiously, sticking the blade of the knife into the sand every few inches, and Indy followed, keeping his arms and legs as close to his body as possible.

Within five yards, the tip of the knife struck something hard. Alistair drew a cautious circle around it with the blade, motioned to Indy, and continued.

"Mines," Indy said.

This process was repeated over and over for the next twenty yards. Alistair seemed calm, and he worked methodically, refusing to be hurried. Sweat dripped from Indy's face onto the sand, and when he could stand it no more, he said: "Let me spell you."

"No," Alistair said. "We've just a little more to go."

The crimson disk of the sun was peeking above the ridge where Indy had left Alecia. He hoped she was gone by now, long gone. It would have seemed a particularly cruel trick of fate to let them get so close to escaping only to thwart them at the last instant, and he remembered what Alecia had said about wanting things too much.

"We've got to make a run for it," Indy said. "There's no time left. Our best hope is to take our chances with the mines, rather than be picked off by the sharpshooters in the towers."

"Have you ever seen what is left of a man who has stepped upon a mine?" Alistair asked. "I'd rather be shot. Besides, just a few yards more—"

Sand sprayed into Indy's face. It was followed a fraction of a second later by the report of a rifle, sharp in the still dawn air and echoing from the surrounding ridges.

A klaxon began to wail behind them.

Indy jerked Alistair to his feet and shoved him forward. They ran for the closest ridge.

In a moment the main gate of the camp swung upon. A half-track emerged, slewing sand as it made a wide turn and bore down upon the pair. A soldier brought the bolts back on a twin .30-caliber gun mounted on top of the armored car.

The pair ran faster, their legs pumping like pistons.

They had almost made it to the rocks when the half-track ground to a stop, blocking their path. Three motorcycles sputtered up behind them. The soldiers in the sidecars had their swivel guns trained on Indy's back.

Indy dropped to his knees, his chest heaving. Alistair leaned on his shoulder to keep from collapsing. "Sorry, old man," Alistair said between breaths. "We gave it a good try."

The soldiers barked orders in Italian.

"I think they want us to put our hands up," Alistair said.

Alistair raised his right hand cautiously in the air, but extended his left to help Indy to his feet. Indy grinned as he took the hand with his own left, and as he came to his feet he brought his right into Alistair's jaw with all the strength he had left.

Alistair went sprawling on his back on the sand.

"There was no minefield," Indy said, his feet planted over Alistair. "The half-track cut right through where we've spent the last thirty minutes crawling on our hands and knees. No wonder you didn't want me to spell you. All you marked were buried rocks."

The gunner at the twin .30s directed a burst near Indy's feet.

"I don't care, go ahead and shoot me," Indy said, jerking a thumb at his chest. "I deserve it. I knew not to trust him, but I bought the minefield story."

Alistair sat up and laughed through a mouthful of blood.

A staff car approached, Italian flags fluttering from the front fenders. Balbo and Sarducci were in the backseat. Sarducci stood as the car came to a halt.

"Bravo," Sarducci said, bringing his gloved hands together. "A stellar performance."

"The latrine." Alistair chuckled. "That's where he was hiding."

"That's really quite good," Sarducci said. "The undeniable call of nature, and all that. Simple, but effective. I, on the other hand, would have devised something a little more . . . elegant."

Balbo sat with his chin in his hands, not speaking, looking annoyed and slightly embarrassed.

"Almost had me out," Alistair said. "The Yank can be quite persuasive. Threatened to break my neck if I called out or otherwise gave him away, and I believed him. So I had to think of something to stall with until the sun came up."

"Aren't you supposed to evaporate in sunlight?" Indy asked.

Balbo suppressed a smile.

"Bind his wrists," Sarducci directed.

One of the motorcycle gunners came forward with

a length of cord and tied Indy's hands tightly behind his back.

Sarducci stepped down from the car.

"Now, let's see. Where is Miss Dunstin hiding?"

Indy laughed.

"Come now, I'm sure she insisted on participating in this little adventure. The excitement has gripped her like a drug, and she couldn't resist the fantasy of saving her brother. Where is she?"

"She's long gone, Sardi," Indy said.

Sarducci shut his eyes.

"Don't call me that," he said. "If he calls me that again, hit him. I'll ask you again, Dr. Jones. Where is Miss Dunstin?"

"Go fish."

The motorcycle gunner backhanded him.

Indy coughed and spat blood.

"The truth, *Indy*," Sarducci demanded.

"She's dead," Indy said.

Alistair looked alarmed.

"And how did she die?" Sarducci asked.

"It was an accident," Indy said. "She slipped and fell on the rocks when we were leaving the ship. There was nothing I could do. Her head was split wide open. She died in my arms."

"He's lying," Sarducci said. "He wouldn't be here if she were dead. Hit him again."

This time it was a hook into the stomach. Indy sank to his knees, vomiting into the sand.

"Pick him up," Sarducci said. "Wipe his mouth. Yes, that's better. Once again, Dr. Jones. Where is Alecia Dunstin? If you lie—well, perhaps you're catching on by now."

"Yeah, she was here," Indy said. "But she took off long before sunrise. You'll never find her. She's got enough supplies to last a week, and a bedouin guide who knows every inch of this country like the back of his hand. Sardi, you're out of luck."

Sarducci nodded.

Another fist to the face.

Indy glared at the gunner. Blood ran from his nose and mouth, and it now took two soldiers to hold him up.

"You wouldn't do that if my hands were free," Indy said, slurring his words.

"Yes," Sarducci said, "and you wouldn't be lying so desperately unless Miss Dunstin were close by. Let's drop the bravado, Dr. Jones, while you are still able to speak."

Balbo called from the car.

"Yes, Italo," Sarducci said. "Just a moment."

"Now," Balbo said in Italian.

Sarducci frowned.

"Air Marshal Balbo, the governor of Libya, is requesting a word with me," Sarducci told the gunner. "Keep him alive until I return. Don't let him sag so heavily between you. Like crucifixion, it taxes the diaphragm and eventually stops respiration."

Sarducci went to the car and listened while Balbo voiced his objection to Indy's treatment. Finally, Balbo exited the car and walked over to Indy.

"Dr. Jones, I am sorry," he said in heavily accented English. He took a handkerchief from his pocket and wiped the blood and saliva from Indy's chin. "I do not approve of this treatment, but Minister Sarducci has a mandate from the chief himself. Politics makes strange bedfellows, no? Sarducci is above human law, or perhaps below it."

Indy squinted to focus his eyes.

"You're shorter than I thought you'd be," he said.

Balbo smiled.

"I have had the chief pretending to be the mastermind of the flight from Rome, and Sarducci running out of control with one of my aircraft," he said. "It has been intolerable. And what do I receive for such unflinching loyalty? To be given a meaningless title and grounded upon this godforsaken expanse of sand and rock."

Balbo sighed.

"Sarducci will kill you, of course," Balbo said as he carefully folded the handkerchief. "I cannot save you. But I can prevent him from mistreating you further. I want you to know, from one soldier to another, that I have for you the greatest respect. You have been an inspiration. And because you have soared above the clouds, at least for a short time with the armada, I would like to offer you one small comfort, if you will allow."

"You bet," Indy said. He no longer tried to focus his eyes.

Balbo unpinned an insignia of silver eagle wings from his own uniform.

"You are *atlantici*," he said, and slipped the insignia into Indy's shirt pocket. He stepped back, clicked his heels together, and threw Indy a salute.

Balbo walked back to the car and Sarducci returned.

"Sardi," Indy said. He explored a loose front tooth with his tongue. "I've only been a fascist ten seconds and already I feel like killing somebody."

"Put him on top of the half-track where she can see him," Sarducci said. The motorcycle soldiers dragged Indy atop the cab. "Now hand me the megaphone. Yes, thank you."

Sarducci climbed onto the hood.

"Miss Dunstin," he called through the megaphone, turning in a circle. His voice echoed back from the rocks. "I know you can hear me. We have your brother and Dr. Jones. Please watch closely."

Sarducci drew the pistol from the flap holster at his belt and fired a round into the air. Then he put the gun to Indy's temple.

"If you don't reveal yourself in one minute, Dr. Jones will die," he called. "But if you do give yourself up, I promise that no harm will come to him. The choice is yours. . . . You now have fifty-five seconds."

"Alecia," Indy shouted. "Don't bel—"

The motorcycle gunner stuffed a rag into Indy's mouth. Indy bit his fingers. Sarducci waited patiently, and the barrel of the gun never wavered.

"Thirty seconds."

The barrel pressed harder against Indy's temple.

"Ten seconds."

Indy tried to think of something pleasant.

"Don't kill him!" a voice called from beyond the rocks. "You win. I give up. Just don't shoot." Alecia stood up, her hands in the air.

Sarducci holstered the pistol and jumped down from the hood of the half-track. He motioned for the soldiers to bring her down to him.

"You were even closer than I thought," Sarducci said. "How nice of you to join us."

"I'm not joining anything," Alecia said, struggling

with the soldiers who held her hands behind her back.
"And I don't know how you could, Alistair Dunstin.
Jones risked his life to save you, and this is how you
repay him? I can't believe we came out of the same
womb."

"It's for a greater good," Alistair said.

"Get Dr. Jones down," Sarducci called. "Chain him
to a bed in the infirmary and treat his wounds. If he is
able to eat, give him whatever he likes. And launder his
clothes, would you? Pin that pair of toy wings to his
breast. He must look his best for his execution in the
morning."

"Execution?" Alecia shrieked.

"Of course," Sarducci said. "Dawn, I think. That is
the customary hour."

"But you promised," she cried.

"My dear," Sarducci chided. "When are you going
to learn to stop *trusting* people?"

Beneath a bloodred sky and clouds the color of gunmetal, Indy stood against a brick wall in one corner of
the camp, his hands behind his back. His clothes were
neatly pressed, his leather jacket was oiled, and his fedora had been cleaned and steamed back into shape.
The cuts on his face had been stitched together and
treated with antiseptic. Twenty yards away eight soldiers
waited at attention with their rifles at their sides.

"You must appreciate the beauty of the thing,"
Sarducci told Indy. "I have distributed eight cartridges
to the squad, all identical in weight and appearance.
They will fire simultaneously, aiming at your heart. But
only four of the cartridges are real; the other half are
harmless blanks. In this way, I hope to ease their minds,

to plant the small and pitiful hope that perhaps they did not fire one of the fatal shots that put an end to their decorated comrade. Very humane, wouldn't you say?"

"Let Alecia go," Indy said.

"Not on your life, as you Americans would say," Sarducci quipped. "She has become a valuable commodity to me, Dr. Jones. Surely you have noted the uncanny resemblance to my late Mona. I must confess that it troubled me for some time, and I pondered the possibilities of reincarnation and the transmigration of souls. But alas, there are no easy answers, and it is a problem I think we must work out together. Ah, there she is now."

Alecia stumbled as Luigi pushed her around the corner of the wall. Her hands were bound in front of her, and she wore a flowing white dress cinched by a golden buckle. Around her neck was a necklace of lapis lazuli.

Alistair was with them. His hands were bound as well.

"Beautiful, isn't she?" Sarducci asked. "I thought it would be nice if she dressed for the occasion."

"Yes," Indy said.

"You'll never have *me*, you maniac," Alecia screamed, struggling against Luigi's iron grip. Her dress billowed in the gathering breeze. "No matter what you do to me, I'll be far away, always out of reach. And the instant you let your guard down, I'll kill you."

"I think we're in for a blow," Sarducci said, glancing at the sky. "But that will soon be none of your concern. Oh, there is one last thing. I would hate for you to go to your final reward without learning the secret of Voynich."

Sarducci snapped his fingers and a *tenente* brought

him a document case. He took the manuscript from it,
and the centuries-old paper riffled in the wind.

"The colors on the manuscript itself," Sarducci
said, "are the clue to its ultimate secret: the location of
the Tomb of Hermes. But that, of course, you know.
What you haven't known is that the solution has been
with you all along, tantalizingly just out of reach."

Sarducci went to Alecia, and as Luigi spun her
around by the shoulders, he grasped the fabric of her
dress and ripped it apart with both hands, revealing
her bare back. The tattoo was even more beautiful than
Indy had imagined; black, red, green, and gold inter-
laced circles and flourishes. The flourishes within the
circles ended in points.

"The key, handed down by generation after generation of metalworkers . . . alchemists," Sarducci said,
indicating the tattoo on Alecia's back. He removed the
glove from his right hand. "Note the interlocking circles
and their shades of color. Quite magnificent. Doesn't
look like a map, but it is. This, in the center. The red
circle with the black dot in the middle. That is Alexandria; at exactly noon of the vernal equinox during the
first year of the second century, a stick cast onto the
ground threw no shadow. This is the reference for all
other points."

Sarducci trailed his middle finger across her back,
the nail leaving an ugly red mark, and Alecia shivered.

"You can find any spot on the surface of the earth
given that constant reference," Sarducci said. "It all de-
pends on the length of the dial and its orientation within
the circle. This green one, for example." He indicated a
circle with a short diallike flourish at twenty-eight degrees. "Cairo. Or rather, the precise representation of a

stick placed perfectly upright at noon on the same day. The Ptolemys, you see, knew the world was round centuries before that myth about Columbus."

Sarducci's finger trailed down Alecia's spine.

"Other locations, of course. Here's Rome. And the tinkers have added a few modern ones to the narrative— London, for example, and Moscow. It doesn't matter where the circles are in relation to one another, all of the information is contained within them."

His finger stopped at a golden circle in the small of Alecia's back. "Here is the prize, the Tomb of Hermes. Roughly on the border between Libya and Egypt, where Alexander found it during his pilgrimage in Siwa. The manuscript gives us the time and date of the reference point—and that, together with Alecia's 'topography,' will soon give me the exact latitude and longitude of the cave. The mathematics are somewhat laborious, but not difficult. Elegant, no?"

Sarducci smiled.

"How can I ever thank you two for bringing her here to me?" he asked.

Alistair looked at the ground.

"Let her go," he said.

"Well, let's get on with it, shall we?" Sarducci asked. "Turn Miss Dunstin around, Luigi, so she can enjoy the show."

Tears streaked Alecia's heavy makeup.

Sarducci withdrew a pack of Lucky Strikes from his pocket.

"Cigarette?" he asked Indy.

"I don't smoke."

"Ah," Sarducci said. "Health reasons. Blindfold?"

"I'm not afraid," Indy said.

"You should be." Sarducci walked away, leaving Indy alone in front of the bullet-marked brick wall. He planted his feet near the firing squad and replaced his glove.

"Ready," Sarducci said.

The firing squad brought their weapons to port arms.

Alecia looked at Indy, and her eyes pleaded forgiveness.

Indy smiled.

"I hate your guts, Princess."

"Oh, Indy," Alecia said. "I hate you, too."

"Aim," Sarducci barked.

Indy swallowed and looked forward. The squad had shouldered their rifles and their fingers were on the triggers. The barrels were pointed at Indy's chest.

Sarducci waited a moment, savoring the tension. He raised his hand with a flourish, prepared to give the final command.

Luigi licked his lips.

Indy closed his eyes.

Sarducci gave the command to fire, but the squad couldn't hear him above the explosion that toppled the guard tower at their corner of the perimeter. Shots erupted beyond the fence, long bursts of automatic-weapons fire, and three of the executioners were knocked from their feet. Mounted bedouins surged over the fence. The other members of the firing squad ran, abandoning, unfired, their single-shot weapons.

Luigi ran with them.

"No," Sarducci screamed. "Come back!" He snatched up one of the rifles, then walked to within point-blank range, took aim at Indy's chest, and fired.

Indy's breath was knocked short as the wax plug of the blank bounced off his sternum.

"That hurt," Indy gasped, then swung the toe of his boot upward between Sarducci's legs. Sarducci buckled, the rifle slipped from his hands, and he dropped to his knees.

"And this is for Alecia," Indy said, kneeing him in the face. Sarducci went over backward in the sand, unconscious.

"Greetings," Prince Farquhar said as he dismounted and cut Indy's hands free with his knife. "You are glad to see me, I presume?"

"You presume right," Indy said.

Riding close behind Farquhar was Sallah, leading a pair of horses.

"Indy, my friend," Sallah called as he slid down from the saddle. "When Captain Marlow told me that he had deposited you here, I came quickly because I knew you would need my assistance."

Sallah wrapped Indy in a bear hug, pulling his feet from the ground. Indy pounded his shoulder, partly out of affection and partly because he couldn't breathe.

"You know the prince?" he asked incredulously.

"But of course," Sallah said. "He is one of my brothers-in-law." Then he leaned close to Indy. "Between you and me, however, it is a very troubling thing. A mixed marriage, you know."

"How long have you been out there?" Indy asked.

"A few hours, only," Farquhar said.

"Hours?" Alecia asked. Her hands were behind her neck, tying her dress together at the collar. "You've been out there for hours? You bloody well waited long enough. I nearly died of fright."

"I performed Dr. Jones a great service by waiting," Farqhuar said as he slit the cord that bound Alecia's hands. "How often do we wonder how we will face death. Will we disgrace ourselves and our families, or will we behave so that when our time comes, Allah welcomes us with open arms? Now Dr. Jones knows."

"I already had a notion," Indy said, rubbing his wrists. "Allah could wait."

Farqhuar laughed.

"Allah waits for no man," he said.

Alistair held out his bound hands.

Farqhuar hesitated.

Indy took the razor-sharp knife and strode over to Alistair, who blinked and drew his hands to his face, thinking Indy was going to plunge the blade into his heart.

Indy severed the cord at his wrists.

"You're free," Indy said. "Choose your side."

The fascists had recovered from the surprise and were now beginning to fight the nomads in earnest. Bullets zipped overhead.

"We must fly," Sallah said.

"There aren't enough horses," Alistair said, looking panicked.

Indy took the document case from Sarducci and pulled Alecia up behind him in the saddle of the whitest of the horses. Sallah shrugged and flicked the reins of the other horse toward Alistair.

With Farqhuar in the lead, they raced toward the broken fence, their horses leaping the jumble of timbers that had been the watchtower. Sallah followed Farqhuar toward the west, but Indy called to him and reined to a stop.

"No," he said.

"But, Indy," Sallah protested.

"We're going this way," Indy said, and he wheeled the horse to the east, toward Egypt.

"Wait," Prince Farqhuar called. He motioned for three of his nomads to follow, then galloped in pursuit. "We have not yet discussed the wonderful autobiography of Huckleberry Finn!"

8

THE STONE

Behind them a plume of dust marked the armored column of the fascists. It had steadily advanced throughout the day, and now it was near enough that Indy could see the glint of the sun from the windshields of the half-tracks.

"Our mounts are no match for their iron beasts," Sallah said, patting the neck of his horse. "We are already in danger of running our animals to their deaths in this unwatered wilderness."

"What do you think, Prince?" Indy asked.

"What Sallah says is true," he said. "But to stop now is to invite dishonor. We must push ahead, no matter what, and trust that Allah will provide."

"I thought they would stop when we crossed the border, rather than risk going to war with Egypt," Indy said.

"Borders," Farquhar said, "mean very little out

here. There are no lines in the sand as there are on your maps. Besides, who would know if they were to rub us out? Some camel driver, perhaps, a thousand years from now."

They rode on, and as time passed and their lathered horses slowed, the distance between them and the ominous plume of dust closed. The sky, which had been dark all day, grew even more threatening, and sand whipped across the dunes.

As they drew abreast of the remains of a ruined temple to a long-forgotten god, Indy's horse stumbled and nearly fell with her double load.

"It is time to stop," the prince said, jumping down from his horse. From a guard on a leather thong, he poured the last of his water into the palm of his hand and allowed his horse to drink. "There you are, Arcturus. Drink. We stick together, don't we? That is the first law of the desert."

"I wish we had more water for the animals," Alecia said, squinting her eyes against the blowing sand.

"It's good that we don't," Sallah observed. "They would drink too greedily, their bellies would swell, and then they would founder and die."

"I wish we had more water for us," Indy said. "Both of the canteens that Sallah brought were pierced by bullets during the raid. There is a little left in the bottom of each, but not much."

The prince was eyeing the ruins of the temple, his mind working. "These stones will provide some protection," he said finally.

"Not much," Alistair observed. "Besides, they will simply circle around us."

"Not protection from the Roman pigs," Farqhuar

said. "From the storm that is coming from the east. Have
you not seen it? When the time comes—and it will
strike with the suddenness of lightning—bring your animals to the ground with you and hold them there."

"You mean a sandstorm?" Indy asked.

"The same."

Indy stepped atop one of the broken columns. The
wind whipped at his clothes and sand danced against the
leather of his jacket like tiny raindrops.

"Do you want the glasses?" Sallah offered.

"I don't need them," he said. "They're less than a
mile away, and coming up fast. Five half-tracks, and a
few trucks. All stuffed with troops, I'm sure."

Farqhuar unslung his Thompson and motioned for
his trio of nomads to take up positions behind the stones.

"It will be decided in a few moments," the prince
said. "Upon which we must fight first—nature or man. If
it be man, then wait until they are close enough to make
every shot count. If it be nature, begin now to ready
your prayers. That is the first law of the desert."

"I thought the first law was sticking together," Indy
said.

Farqhuar smiled.

The wind blew stiffly and then suddenly died.

"Look," Alecia said, pointing to the east.

A dark cloud rolled across the desert floor, seem-
ingly in slow motion. In the other direction, the fascist
column had drawn close enough that Indy could read
the unit numbers on the hoods of the half-tracks.

The column ground to a halt. Then the front wheels
of the lead half-track turned, and the vehicle cut a circle
in the sand as it raced in the opposite direction. The
other vehicles followed, pell-mell.

"They're going to try and outrun it," Indy said.

"The horses," Sallah said. "Get them down and lie upon their necks."

Farqhuar wrapped a rag around his nose and mouth, then grasped the bridle of Arcturus and slowly twisted his neck until the animal dropped to the sand. The others followed his example, and by the time the last animal was down, the storm was upon them with the force of a freight train.

Indy tucked his hat into his jacket and held Alecia tight against him as they lay behind their horse. The sand was everywhere, driven by the wind into their eyes and mouths, their nostrils, and especially their ears.

"I'm suffocating," Alecia said.

"Don't think about it," Indy told her. "Keep your head down and make a pocket in the crook of your arm to breathe."

Even in the protection afforded by the lee side of the temple stones, the sand piled high around them, threatening to bury them alive. Indy used his hands to shovel the sand away from them, but it was like trying to empty a swimming pool with a teacup.

In seven minutes the storm was gone.

Indy struggled from beneath a mound of sand, pulling Alecia up after him. He slapped her on the cheek and she gasped for breath.

"Are you both all right?" Sallah asked, brushing the sand from his clothes.

"Yes, I think so," Indy said.

Alecia and Indy's white horse rose to her feet, hundreds of pounds of sand sloughing from her back. Indy patted her flank affectionately.

"Where's Alistair?" Alecia asked.

"Here," he called, raising a hand in the air. "My horse is quite dead, however."

Prince Farqhuar squatted upon a heap of sand, his face in his hands. "One of my men is dead," he said. "The desert has claimed as well poor Arcturus, star of the west."

"What about the column?" Alistair asked.

Indy climbed the stones again and surveyed the desert with the binoculars. Sallah stepped up beside him.

"What do you see?" he asked.

"Nothing," Indy said. "Absolutely nothing. There's not a trace left of them."

"The desert," Farqhuar said as he and his remaining two nomads began digging the corpse of the third from the sand. "It gives, it takes. It hides some, it reveals others. Always, it is changing."

"If only we knew where we were," Indy said.

"I'm sorry that I cannot help you," Farqhuar said. "This is an area that my people rarely venture into, for the reason that those who do are seldom seen again."

"But, Indy," Sallah said. "We are about ten kilometers on the Egyptian side of the border, give or take a few. That much even I can tell, from the direction we traveled and the speed we made."

"I mean precisely," Indy said. "I know we are within fifteen miles of the general location of the Tomb of Hermes—which, tradition has it, is near an oasis—but that amounts to more than two hundred square miles of desert."

"You make life too difficult for yourself, Indy," Sallah said. "Why did you not say what you mean in the first place? Before leaving Cairo, I gathered a few items that I thought we might need: maps, a compass, a bottle of brandy. For medicinal purposes, only."

"Sallah, I could kiss you," Indy said.

"I would prefer that you did not," Sallah said gravely as he retrieved the compass and the tube of survey maps from his saddlebag.

Indy examined the maps, found the one he wanted, and unrolled it on one of the fallen slabs of rock. He placed a stone at each corner of the curled map.

"This map has very little detail, but it has enough," he said. "Look here. These two highest peaks. Their latitude and longitude."

Alistair turned to orient himself to the map, then pointed to the north. "There is one of the peaks," he said. Then he gestured to the southwest. "There is the other."

"Good," Indy said. He retrieved his field notebook from the lining of the jacket and drew the pencil from beneath the rubber band. Then he opened the azimuth compass, leveled it, and took a reading. He jotted down the degrees. Then he took a reading from the second peak and recorded it as well. "I need the protractor and the straightedge."

Sallah retrieved the needed items.

After adjusting for deviation from true north, Indy reckoned the degrees with the protractor, then used the ruler to draw a line south from the first mountain peak. Another line went northeast from the second peak.

"We're here, where the lines cross," Indy said.

"So far so good, Indy," Sallah said. "We know with certainty where we are. But how are we going to find the tomb, if it is not on the map? We must know the exact location of both points before we can plot a course."

Indy looked across the map at Alecia.

"We need to borrow your back," he said.

Alecia reached behind her neck and untied the knot holding her dress together. The back fell away while she held it gathered in the front.

"Alistair," Indy said. "You'd better help me with this. I know I can get the measurements, but I'm not sure what to do with them."

"It might take me a bit," Alistair said, "but yes, I think I can work them out."

Alecia jumped when Indy laid the instruments against her skin.

"Sorry," he said.

Indy scribbled the required information in the notebook, then handed it to Alistair. He took Indy's pencil and sat down on the slab, scratching his beard with the eraser.

"You know how long I've been waiting for this information?" Alistair asked as he worked. "And I never knew. I suppose the best place to hide something, as they say, is in plain sight."

"My back," Alecia said, "is not exactly plain sight."

"Sorry," Alistair said. "But really, we did grow up together. I caught glimpses of it every now and then, probably more so than you did, because I don't ever recall your using a pair of mirrors to examine your dorsal self with."

Alistair filled the page with calculations, then went on to the next. Every so often he would stop, make a face, and erase a column. Occasionally he would pare away at the point of the pencil with his pocketknife to make it serviceable again. When he was finally through, and had written the degrees, minutes, and seconds upon the map, the pencil was not much more than a stub.

"There we are," Alistair said.

Indy looked at the coordinates, then used the dividers to mark an X in a particularly rugged piece of terrain. He drew a line from the X to their position, then measured the angle and the distance.

"Do you think you calculated correctly?" Indy asked.

"Rather," Alistair said. "If I hadn't, it wouldn't have put the location of the tomb in our laps."

"Alecia," Indy said, "I don't mean to be indelicate, but did Sarducci take any photographs, or make any sketches?"

"Of my back?" she asked. "No, not at all."

"Good," he said. "Then we shouldn't be followed, even if he managed to escape becoming part of the terrain."

"Do you think that's a possibility?" Alistair asked.

Indy looked at him.

"Unless somebody shows me that bald head on a plate," Indy said, "it will be something I will think about for the rest of my life."

"Quite," Alistair said.

"We're less than twelve kilometers away," Indy explained to the rest. "Sallah, I want you to take the compass and keep us on a steady course of forty-seven degrees. It won't be as easy to find as it sounds, however, because the tomb is in a protected valley. We might have to search for some time, do some climbing, and clear some debris. Prince, do you think we could employ your men as diggers?"

"Find me an oasis," Farqhuar said, being careful to speak in English, "and you can roast them for lunch."

In three hours the seven had reached the sheltered valley and entered it by following an ancient footpath that wound among the cliffs. Indy was in the lead, walking the white horse carefully down the narrow trail.

"There's something here," he said. "These paths were made by workmen. Very similar to what you find in the Valley of the Kings. And look at those piles of rubble. They aren't natural—it's refuse, shards of chipped rock that have been dumped about the valley in an effort to disguise what went on here."

"I can't tell any difference between this terrain and everything we've passed since leaving Libya," Alecia said. "Indy, you must have good eyes."

"Thanks to Sallah," Indy said. "He's the one who taught me to read these signs. It's not the kind of thing you get out of books, you know."

The white horse had suddenly become difficult, pawing at the ground and fighting Indy's hand on her bridle. Indy patted her neck in an attempt to calm her, but his heels skidded on the narrow path as the horse pulled him forward.

"What's wrong with her?" Alecia asked.

"She smells water," Sallah said.

Indy let the horse lead him around the next corner, which allowed a clear view of the valley. Below was the oasis, a shimmering pool ringed by palms. A pair of crows cackled from atop the tallest tree.

"We made it," he said.

.   .   .

Indy lounged in the shadow of a palm tree, his back against the rough bark of the trunk, eating a date. Sallah sat beside him, nibbling on a fig.

"This is indeed a paradise," Sallah said.

Indy murmured his agreement. He was watching Alecia as she knelt at the edge of the pool, her legs folded beneath her, washing the grit from her face.

"It could be a picture from the Bible," Indy observed.

"This Englishwoman. She means something to you?"

"Something," Indy replied.

"I apologize for being so rude," Sallah said. "You are reluctant to discuss it."

"You're not rude," Indy said, and placed his hand on Sallah's shoulder. "I'm just not in the mood right now. But it is something that I'd like your advice on when we are safely back. I may even need your help."

"Anything," Sallah said. "You need only to ask."

Alecia was sitting on the top step of what looked like a row of stairs going down into the water. She dipped her feet in the water and uttered a sigh of relief. She glanced around her, hesitant for a moment, and then she lowered herself into the pool. When the water had reached her shoulders, she slipped her dress over her head and threw it on the bank.

"Give me your reading on this place," Indy said. "It's been troubling me since we first spotted the oasis."

"Very well," Sallah said, selecting a date from the pile beside Indy. "There has obviously been much work done here. I have been studying the cliff faces, but I can see none of the usual places where a tomb would be hidden—a natural crevice in the rocks, for example."

"I agree."

"What strikes me as odd," Sallah said, "is the oasis itself. It is the work of man, not of nature. There should *be* no oasis here. And the water itself—it is unnaturally warm, as if it were heated in the bowels of the earth. Then there is the matter of the stone steps—a journey leading to nowhere."

"Perhaps not," Indy said. "The Indians of the American plains believed that pools of water were gateways to the spirit world. Perhaps the steps lead to a doorway."

"Intriguing," Sallah said. "So you propose to swim to the bottom to find this door."

"Yes."

Sallah's face darkened.

"Alas," he said. "I cannot swim. It never occurred to me that it would be a skill I would someday need, having made my life in sand and rock. I am afraid that I will not be able to accompany you, my friend."

"Sallah," Indy said, standing and brushing the seeds from his pants, "you will be with me always, wherever I go." He retrieved a blanket from Sallah's stockpile in the saddlebag and carried it to the edge of the water. "Enjoying yourself?" he asked Alecia.

"It is wonderful," she said, crossing her arms over her chest. "You should try it. After I'm out, of course."

"I brought you this," Indy said, indicating the blanket. "It's a little rough, but I thought you could wear it until your dress is dry. Are you ready?"

Indy grasped the blanket by the corners and held it in front of him, his head turned, while Alecia crawled gracefully out of the water and stepped into it. She wrapped it around her, tucking the ends tightly over her chest.

Indy unlaced his boots. He placed them together on the top step, with his socks inside. Then he unbuttoned his shirt and slipped off his belt.

Wearing only his trousers, he walked down the steps until the water was up to his waist. He paused for a moment, filling his lungs with air.

"I'll be right back," he said, then took a last gulp of air and held it.

"Where do you think you're going?" Alecia asked.

Indy dove forward.

He kicked downward, following the steps, using his hands to help pull himself along. The weight of the water pressed against his ears, telling him he was passing ten or twelve feet, and he worked his jaw to equalize the pressure in his eustachian tubes.

The water was clear and the rays of the late-afternoon sun shimmered over the steps. His eyes did not sting, as they would have in seawater, and he had no trouble following the staircase. The pool was surprisingly deep, and Indy had to clear his ears once more before finding that the steps led into the mouth of an underwater cave.

Indy darted beneath the lip of the opening, trailing his hand against the rock, then kicked upward. He proceeded cautiously, feeling his way with his hands now that he had lost most of the light, being careful not to slam against an unexpected outcropping.

Suddenly he broke the surface.

He shook his head, clearing the water from his eyes, and looked around him. In the dim light that filtered up from the bottom of the pool, he saw that he

was in a vast subterranean chamber. The steps led out of
the water to a carved stone archway. A figure loomed in
the darkness below the archway, a statue or something,
but he could not make out what it was.

Beyond was darkness.

Indy rested for a moment on the steps, half out of
the water. The chamber echoed with the sound of water
dripping into the pool from his upper body, and it
seemed as if the eyes of the stone figure beneath the
archway were on the back of his neck. When his breathing had returned to normal, he dove back into the water
and returned.

"Indy," Alecia said. "You nearly scared me to death.
You were gone so long that I thought you had drowned."

"Indy, what did you find?" Sallah asked. The prince
was with him, waiting expectantly.

"This is the entrance," he said. "The cave is at the
bottom of the pool, and there are more steps leading
through an arched doorway. But I couldn't see much
because it was too dark."

"You need torches," Sallah said. "We can strip the
fibrous bark from the palms and bind it together with
rags. Prince, do your men carry any grease for their
weapons, or pitch to dress the wounds of their horses?"

"Of course," Farqhuar said.

"We can soak the ends of our torches with both,"
Sallah said. "They will not be perfect, and they will give
much smoke, but they should be adequate. I will coat
the ends of some matches with candle wax so you may
light the torches when you emerge on the other side."

Farqhuar spoke to his nomads in tarog, command-
ing them to start gathering materials.

"Where's Alistair?" Indy asked.

"He's studying some birds he found in the trees over there," Alecia said.

"Birds? What kind of birds?" Indy asked. He looked worried.

"I'm not sure," Alecia said.

"Can he swim?"

"He swims quite well," she answered.

"Then I need him," Indy said. "Make enough torches for two, Sallah. Hurry."

"Shouldn't you wait until first light?" Sallah asked.

"Where we're going," Indy said, "it won't matter."

Indy emerged in the chamber with his shoes slung around his neck and the bundle of torches beneath his arm. Alistair popped to the surface a moment later, gasping and spitting water.

Indy struck one of Sallah's matches and held it beneath one of the torches. The torch sizzled, a flame appeared, then died. On the third match, the flame finally held, and he used that torch to give life to Alistair's.

Indy quickly laced his shoes and slipped into his shirt, which had been wrapped along with his field notebook in a bit of oilcloth that the nomads had produced.

Holding their torches aloft, he and Alistair approached the archway. The stone figure beneath seemed to dart and feint in the flickering light. The statue was that of a man, life-sized, with a flowing beard. His robes were covered with alchemical symbols: the sun and moon, the stars, winged Mercury. His right hand was raised palm out in a gesture of warning, while his left beckoned the travelers forth.

"Remarkable," Alistair said. "The thrice-great Hermes."

"Gives me the spooks," Indy said.

Indy recited the Coptic inscription above the arch: "Behold the threshold. The call is answered. The journey begins with knowledge, but ends with faith. V-I-T-R-I-O-L." He paused. "That last mean anything to you?"

"*Visita Interiora Terraie, Rectificando, Inveniens Occultum Lapidem,*" Alistair said. " 'Visit the interior parts of the earth, and by rectifying you will discover the hidden stone.' "

They walked beneath the arch and found themselves in a twelve-sided hall. There seemed to be no exit. In an alcove set into each of the sides was a relief that represented an alchemical process. The reliefs were dominated by furnaces and alembics, flasks and retorts. The floor was made up of an interlocking mosaic of six-sided stones. Each stone had one of the twelve zodiacal symbols carved upon it.

Alistair took a step forward and the stone under his foot plunged beneath him. Indy caught him by the collar and hauled him back. The missing stone left a man-sized shaft that was twelve feet deep.

"Careful," he said. "Think about what you're doing. These zodiacal symbols on the floor. Can they be arranged in any sequence other than by month?"

"Of course," Alistair said. "The alchemical sequence. Each symbol stands for a process."

"Then we'll take it in order," Indy said.

"Calcination is first," Alistair said. "That's Aries."

They stepped together onto the stone with the symbol for the ram. The entire floor sank, leaving the stone they were standing upon a foot above the others.

"Is it safe?" Alistair asked.

"We're still here, aren't we?" Indy asked. "Next?"

"Congelation. Taurus."

They stepped down upon the bull. The stones rumbled and sank another foot, leaving Taurus halfway between the floor and Aries at the threshold.

"It's making a stairway down," Indy said. "Go ahead."

Next was Gemini, for fixation, followed by Cancer, for dissolution. Then came Leo, Virgo, and Libra—digestion, distillation, and sublimation—and Scorpio for separation. The floor was now eight feet below the threshold, and the top of a doorway had appeared above the floor.

When Sagittarius through Pisces had been chosen —representing ceration, fermentation, multiplication, and projection—the doorway was fully revealed. The twelve stones that had been chosen remained at various heights, stairstepping their way up to the threshold.

"It's like being at the bottom of a well," Alistair said.

"Wells don't have stairs," Indy said. "So far, so good, but it's bound to get harder. And I don't like the inscription above the door: the Path of Trials."

They brushed the cobwebs from the doorway and stepped through into a long, narrow passage. It turned at twenty yards, then sloped downward, and took another turn, winding always downward.

"It reminds me of the type of passage you find inside a pyramid," Indy said.

"This *is* a pyramid, only inverted," Alistair said. "It should end in an apex-shaped chamber."

" 'That Which Is Above Is Below,' " Indy recalled.

"These gouges on the floor and wall are curious, however."

"Marks of the stonecutters?" Alistair suggested.

"No, they're relatively fresh. A few hundred years old, at most." Indy paused. "I've got a bad feeling about them."

They turned a corner and the passage ended in a blank wall. Indy handed his torch to Alistair, then ran the fingers of both hands along the stone, searching for a seam. There was none. Then he tapped on the wall.

"Solid," he said.

"What's this white material hanging against the wall?" Alistair asked, holding the torch up to it. "It has a strange green glow to it. There's a heap of it on the floor as well."

Indy examined his hands, then tasted the residue that clung to his fingertips from touching the wall.

"Calcium," he said. "Phosphorus. Or rather, powdered bone." He touched the pile on the floor with his shoe, and the pile shifted and diminished, draining through a funnel-type hole in the floor, like sand through an hourglass.

"Listen," Indy said.

Something rumbled behind them. The floor began to quiver.

"Whatever it is," Indy said, "it can't be good."

The sound grew louder. Something was scraping and sliding down the corridor, the frightening sound of stone against stone. They waited, their eyes riveted to the last corner they had turned. Dust fell from the ceiling, shaken loose by the vibration.

"We've got to get out of here," Alistair said. "Let's run for it."

Indy held him back.

"Wait," he said.

The sound was like thunder now.

Indy went to the corner and dared a glance. A huge stone filled the passage, advancing inch by inch.

"Okay," he said, moving the torch along the walls, searching for something, anything. "We're trapped in a giant mortar and pestle and are about to be ground up and drained through a hole in the floor, leaving only bone dust."

"That's one way to reduce the human body to its chemical components," Alistair said. "What do we do?"

"We know we can't wait here against the wall," Indy said, "or we'll end up like him. Them. Whatever. Let's walk *toward* the thing and see what happens."

"Toward it?"

"It's taking too long to get here—whoever designed this is trying to make us afraid out of our minds, cowering by the wall, waiting for death. So let's do the unexpected. Greet death."

"Yes, of course," Alistair said. "The wise man welcomes death, the fool fears it."

They walked forward, torches raised, and turned the ninety-degree corner. The pestle was three yards away and rumbling toward them. Indy examined the back wall.

"This is the only place in the passage that hasn't had grooves gouged out of it," he said. Then he held his torch low, examining the floor.

"No bone dust," Indy said. "Here's where we stand. As it closes in on us, it will seem the only direction we can go is back to the wall at the end of the passage, but don't, no matter what happens."

The stone had passed the edge of the corner, narrowing the space in which they stood. It was now three feet away and coming closer. They tossed away their torches. At two feet, Alistair shifted nervously. At one foot, as the stone touched their clothes, he made a move to slide out of the way, but Indy gripped his arm.

The stone touched their chests, and what began as the lightest of pressures quickly became intolerable. Indy's face was turned, and the rough surface of the pestle pressed against his cheek. It felt as if the life were being squeezed out of him.

"I could have been wrong," Indy said.

There was a thud as something fell into place and the wall behind them began to move backward, easing the pressure on their chests. They were plunged into darkness as the stone hid the last of the light from the torches. The pestle's motion changed, and instead of coming forward, it slid to the left, toward the blank wall.

Standing motionless in the darkness, Indy no longer felt the stone wall against his back, and he felt a wisp of air on his neck. He took another torch from the bundle, struck a match, and lit it.

The wall was gone, revealing a passage that sloped gently downward. At the end of the passage they could hear the murmur of running water.

They emerged in another chamber, resembling a Greek temple set above a pond. The water flowed from one end of the pond and disappeared down a twisting series of baffles at the other, cascading into the earth. In the center of the pond, on a pedestal, was a stone lion, with unusually flared nostrils.

Indy dipped his hand in the water.

"It's hot," he said.

"What do you think these baffles are for?" Alistair asked.

"I think they act like some sort of radiator, to dissipate the heat," Indy said, walking around the perimeter of the pond. "Obviously it's fed by some sort of superheated underground river. We're deep enough into the earth now that the temperature should be a constant sixty-four degrees, but it's not. In here, it's positively balmy."

"There's obviously no passage at the bottom of this pool," Alistair said. "If there were, the water level couldn't rise above the lip of the baffles."

"Look around," Indy said. "There must be some other way we're meant to continue. I feel air coming from somewhere."

Indy held the torch aloft and watched as the flame flickered. Then he went to the opposite side of the pond, stepped behind the Doric columns, and inspected the wall. The torch burned a brighter orange.

"It has got to be along this wall," Indy said.

"Hello," Alistair said.

"What have you got?"

"A fellow traveler," Alistair said, holding the torch over a skeleton slumped against the wall. The jawbone hung in a crooked grin beneath the skull. "Twelfth century, judging from the clothes."

"Any sign of what killed him?"

"No," Alistair said, gently probing the fragile cloth. "No indication of being crushed, or shot with an arrow, or any type of violent trauma."

"That's bad," Indy said. "Come over here and tell me what you make of this."

He was standing in front of the stone orb protruding from the wall. Carved into it was the acronym VIT-RIOL.

"Do we push it or pull it or what?" Alistair asked, scratching his beard. "If we want to keep going down, do we push it down?" With both hands, he pushed downward on the orb. It dropped a few inches.

Something began to hiss behind them.

Gas billowed from the lion's nostrils. The air was filled with the stench of rotten eggs.

"Vitriol," Indy said. "Sulfuric acid. Hold your breath. Douse your torch. We've got to get out of here before we are poisoned or blown to bits."

Alistair stamped on his torch, putting it out, and Indy did the same. They were left in darkness, listening to the hiss of the gas as it filled the chamber.

Indy grasped the orb and tried to move it, but it would not budge.

"Down on the floor," he said.

As he crawled on his hands and knees along the wall, Indy's nostrils picked up a whiff of fresh air. He stopped, smelling the air like a bloodhound, trying to determine the direction. His hands searched the base of the wall, and when he touched one section it unexpectedly moved inward.

"Here," he called in the darkness. "I've found it."

Indy crawled into the shaft, followed by Alistair, who was holding on to a belt loop in the back of Indy's pants.

"Must be some type of air passage," Indy commented.

They went forward on their hands and knees. They had gone only a few yards when the shaft began to tilt, turning downward at an alarming rate.

"It must be cantilevered somehow," Indy said. "Triggered by the weight of our bodies. Use your back and legs to jam in the shaft."

The shaft continued to turn until it became vertical instead of horizontal. Indy was well wedged in the shaft, but Alistair did not have a good purchase on the walls and began to slip. He slid down against Indy.

"Get up," Indy said. "I can't hold both of us."

"I'm trying," Alistair said, "but it's too difficult. I'm not a mountain climber. What can we do?"

"This," Indy said as Alistair's rear pressed down upon his head and the soles of his shoes began to slide down the wall, "is the faith part, I think." He let go and plunged down the shaft, dropping through the darkness, with Alistair above him.

The shaft twisted first one way and then another, and they tumbled like marbles down a chute. The shaft gently curved and became horizontal again, but before they could slow their momentum, they passed through a warm waterfall and spilled out into yet another chamber.

Indy lay on the floor, his head spinning.

Alistair sat up and held his head with his hands.

"Indy," he said.

"What?" Indy snapped. "Your feet nearly beat me to death."

"We're there," Alistair said.

Indy looked up, and the chamber slowly stopped swaying. They were inside the apex, the tip of the inverted pyramid, and it was half-filled with water. They were in a sort of causeway that led to a twenty-four-sided solid in the center of the chamber. Above the polyhedron, seeming to float in the darkness, was a glass sarcophagus.

"The Tomb of Hermes," Indy said. He got to his feet and walked carefully down the causeway.

The polyhedron was made up of what seemed to be leaden panels, and three of the panels, spaced equally around the middle, bore recessed handholds inside of a golden circle that seemed to be the end of a tube. The tubes corresponded to three leaden cylinders in a rack on the floor. Indy touched the polyhedron with his hand, and he could feel a soft vibration travel up his arm to his shoulder.

"It feels alive," he said.

"It is beating in time with the universe," Alistair said, laying both hands upon it. "The one true song, the force that binds everything together."

"The torches," Indy said. "We don't need them."

The chamber was filled with a mistlike purple glow.

Through the dark panes of the sarcophagus that floated above, they could see a mummified figure sitting on a throne, a tablet clutched in one skeletal hand. Indy was close enough now to see that the sarcophagus stood on a thin pedestal of some pale bluish material.

"Cobalt?" Indy asked.

"Beryllium, I think," Alistair said, and grasped one of the handholds in the polyhedron. "These are obviously meant to be turned."

"Don't," Indy said. "What is it the Tabula Smaragdina says about opening the vault? That you will be stricken as you stand? Look at the floor."

There were footprints in the floor, one to each side of each of the three panels with the recessed handholds. There were no footprints in front of the panels.

"You're not supposed to stand directly in front of it," Indy said.

Alistair nodded.

They took up positions on either side of the panel. Alistair reached over and grasped the handle.

"Are you really sure we want to do this?" Indy asked.

"I've been waiting my entire life for this moment," Alistair said. His eyes shone. "We are about to discover the philosopher's stone. Do you realize what kind of power and wealth that entails? You can play the fool if you'd like, Jones, but not me."

A familiar laugh made Indy's blood turn to ice water.

Leonardo Sarducci stood at the end of the causeway, a pistol in his hand. His uniform was ragged and his boots were scuffed. Behind him was Luigi with Farqhuar's Thompson submachine gun.

"Please, Dr. Jones," he said. "Play the fool. You do it so well."

"Not again," Indy said.

"Again," Luigi ordered. "For the last time. I will kill you slowly, I will peel your skin from—"

"Later," Sarducci snapped.

"Where are the others?" Indy asked.

"Mona and the others are locked safely inside my vehicle," Sarducci said. "I'm sorry to say that it is the only half-track I have left, following the sandstorm. Luigi and I were lucky enough to have been a few miles behind the column when the storm struck, although it took us nearly a full day to shovel ourselves out of the sand."

Sarducci strode down the walkway, followed by Luigi, and came to a stop directly in front of the handle Alistair was about to turn.

"Proceed, Alistair," Sarducci said. "You should have the honor of being first to open the vault. After all, you're the reason we're all here, aren't you?"

"The birds," Indy said.

"Yes, the birds. Homing pigeons trained to find not a location, but a person—me. Something Alistair bred in his spare time. Inventive, isn't he?"

"Dunstin," Indy snarled.

Alistair scratched his beard.

"Well, yes," he said. "The fascists, you know, are going to win—in Libya, in Ethiopia, everywhere. It will be a new world order. Power is absolute, Dr. Jones. It is best that Alecia and I are on the winning side."

"Even if you break her heart in order to do it," Indy said.

"I need her," Alistair said.

Alistair gripped the handle and rotated it ninety degrees. The sarcophagus floated downward, the beryllium rod disappearing into the polyhedron. The misty purple glow subsided, then all but died. The waterfall over the entrance to the chamber slowed and finally dribbled to a stop.

"Amazing!" Sarducci exclaimed. "Such power, and no moving parts except for a beryllium rod."

"You don't know what you're dealing with," Indy said.

"That's precisely why it intrigues me," Sarducci said.

Alistair tried removing the cylinder, but it wouldn't come. He rotated it further, to one hundred and eighty degrees, and he felt the cylinder become free. He began to slide it out of the polyhedron. As he did, the humming began to subside.

Indy glanced at his feet. His shoes covered the footprints on the floor. He stood as still as stone.

"It's heavy," Alistair said, his feet shuffling.

"It should be," Sarducci said. "If I'm correct, it's made of gold. Luigi, help him."

Luigi shouldered the machine gun and stepped forward, grasping the golden cylinder and pulling it toward him. As the end came free a brilliant shaft of purple light shot from the opening in the polyhedron, as if a furnace door had been opened to reveal a mock sun. Then something dropped down inside the furnace and covered the opening.

Luigi laid the golden cylinder at Sarducci's feet.

"The prize!" Sarducci exclaimed. "The golden casket! Now replace the cylinder with one from the rack, if you please. We mustn't leave without feeding the beast."

Alistair lugged one of the lead cylinders over to the polyhedron, but paused for a moment. He unscrewed the end and reached inside. He withdrew his hand, letting the material slip through his fingers. "As I suspected," he said. "Rich in uranium." Then he replaced the cap and, with Luigi's help, fitted it back into the vacant slot. He locked the handle in place.

The sarcophagus rose once more, exposing the beryllium rod, and the glow was restored to the chamber. Water began to cascade over the entrance once more.

"Now, won't you accompany us to the surface?" Sarducci invited. "I know I should kill you here, but I cannot stand the thought of Mona missing your final moments. You two say such rude things to each other at such times."

.   .   .

The rear door of the half-track swung open and Alecia blinked against the morning sunlight. Indy was shoved inside, his hands bound together, and he landed on his knees at her feet.

"Are you hurt?" Sallah asked.

"I'll live," Indy said.

"Ah, but not for long," Luigi taunted, crawling into the vehicle behind him, the Thompson at the ready. "As soon as the maestro has completed his experiment, you are mine. My brothers will be avenged."

"Something to look forward to," Indy said.

"The Roman pigs have already killed my men," Farqhuar said, glaring at Luigi. "They will pay, tenfold for each life. My nation will—"

Luigi struck him with the butt of the gun. The prince did not cry out.

"Your nation," he said, sneering, "consists of a band of forty ragged nomads. Oh, I'm sorry. Make that thirty-eight. Or is it thirty-seven now?"

Luigi took a seat opposite the four and swigged water from a canteen. He was looking fatigued, and his face and hands were badly sunburned. Indy did not remember the burn when he and Sarducci had appeared in the chamber.

"This experiment," Alecia asked. "Transmutation?"

"Yes," Luigi answered slowly. "The chief will have all of the gold he desires. We fascists, you see, are long on ambition but somewhat short of cash."

Luigi had seemed to lose his characteristic bravado. He closed his eyes for a moment, as if he was too tired to continue talking.

"Soon," he said wearily, "we will be unstoppable."

"You're dying," Indy said. "You know that, don't

you? You stood in front of the furnace. You weren't supposed to do that."

"Lies," Luigi sneered, then hesitated. "I am going to check with the maestro."

He stumbled out of the half-track. Almost as an afterthought, he took a lug wrench and jammed it beneath the door handle, sealing the others inside.

Outside, Sarducci had placed the golden cylinder on the ground and was kneeling before it, struggling with the top. His strength seemed to have left him.

"I'm not sure this is a good idea," Alistair said, wiping a sleeve across his brow. "Perhaps we should wait until we get it to a laboratory, where we can control—"

"Shut up!" Sarducci said. "I must know, and I must know now. Help me."

"No," Alistair said. He sat wearily down, a few yards away.

"Help me," Sarducci barked as Luigi came up.

Luigi put down the gun and together they twisted on the end of the cylinder. Slowly the cap began to turn. Suddenly it turned easily, and Sarducci spun it with both of his gloved hands. When several inches of golden thread were visible, the cap slipped off and fell heavily in the sand.

"The philosopher's stone," Sarducci announced, and withdrew a glowing rod of the purest red. It pulsated with energy as he clutched it to his stomach. He felt its warmth, and as the stone touched the silver buttons of his jacket, each turned a brilliant golden color. "Look," he said breathlessly.

He handed the stone to Luigi, then snatched off the glove of his right hand and searched his uniform for another item of metal to test. Then he remembered his

pistol, withdrew it from its holster, and touched its barrel lightly against the stone. A golden wave traveled
along the blue steel, from the barrel to the frame, leaving only the wooden grip untouched.

Sarducci laughed with glee.

"Maestro," Luigi said. "What is happening to my
hands?"

His fingers had begun to smoke. The skin sagged
and the flesh melted, revealing the bones, and the stone
fell through Luigi's useless fingers. The melting continued, turning the palms to dripping jelly and advancing
up each wrist.

Luigi screamed.

"Help me," he cried in horror as what remained of
his hands dropped away. The melting crawled up each
arm toward his shoulders with agonizing slowness.

Sarducci placed the shining yellow pistol against
Luigi's temple and pulled the trigger. The golden slug
lodged deep into his brain. The barrel of the gun, now
turned to the softest of metals, had burst like a peeled
banana. The armless body fell heavily into the sand and
continued to liquefy. Luigi's clothes burst into flames.

Sarducci threw aside the gun and examined the fingers of his bare right hand. They, too, had begun to
smoke. The flesh had already sloughed away at the tips,
revealing the glistening white bone.

He stumbled to the half-track and, with his good
hand, jerked down the ax that was clamped to the side of
the vehicle. Then he fell to the ground and began to
hack away at his forearm, well above the dripping hand.

Alistair lurched to his feet and walked to the door of
the half-track.

"Alecia," he called. "I'm going to free the door for

you. But you have to promise not to come out, not for a long while. Not until everything has been quiet for a long time."

"Dunstin," Indy demanded. "What's going on?"

Alistair swallowed. It was difficult to talk.

"Don't make me explain," he said. "You don't want to know. Just promise to wait. Alecia, I'm sorry. Someday I hope you can forgive me."

"Alistair," she called. "What are you doing?"

"One last process," he said, managing a smile. "Rectification."

He unjammed the lug wrench.

Then he painfully removed his shirt and wrapped the fabric around his right hand. He knelt, picked up the stone, and slipped it back inside the golden cylinder. It seemed to take him hours to screw the cap back on.

He struggled with the cylinder, dragging it to the edge of the steps leading down into the pool. Then he sighed and looked around. There was no sign of Luigi's body, or of Sarducci. A pair of crows called raucously from the top of the highest palm.

Alistair clutched the cylinder with both hands and tumbled down the steps into the water.

When they could no longer stand the afternoon heat inside the half-track, Indy cautiously swung open the door and stepped outside.

"Where are they?" Alecia asked.

Indy saw the marks in the sand leading to the edge of the pool and knew at least part of the answer. The broken golden gun, and the golden buttons and belt buckle from Sarducci's uniform, glistened in the sand.

Sallah reached down to pick up the buckle, but Indy grasped his hand.

"I wouldn't," he said.

"That's all?" Alecia asked, tears welling in her blue eyes. "They're just gone? Not even a body left behind to bury?"

Indy took her in his arms and held her tightly against him. She cried against his shoulder, letting the tears come unchecked for once.

"Alistair left something far more important," he said, staring at the rut cut into the sand by the cylinder, and Alistair's heel marks where he struggled with it. "He left the memory of finally doing the right thing."

"Allah will be pleased," the prince said.

"Search the half-track for some explosives," Indy said. "Knowing Sarducci, I'm sure he brought some. Let's seal this paradise once and for all."

Sallah nodded, then paused.

"Indy," Sallah said. "There are many things here which I do not understand, but the question which troubles me most is: What is the first matter? What was in the cylinder of lead that fed the beast?"

Indy scooped up a handful of desert and threw it to the wind.

"Sand," he said.

Epilogue

"And that is what you are going to tell the FBI?" Marcus Brody asked as he and Indy passed through the double doors of the Museum of Antiquity. "That there was nothing to any of it? The Tomb of Hermes does not exist, Voynich is gibberish, and the philosopher's stone is simply a dream?"

"A bad dream, Marcus."

"It's almost over," Brody said.

"Thank you for bringing the money so quickly," Indy said. "You don't know what this means to me. Alecia is waiting for me in London."

"My pleasure, Indy. The skull will be a stunning addition to the Central American exhibit," Brody said. "Actually, I'm not surprised that Mussolini went for the deal. With Sarducci dead, he no longer has a stake in all of this. And as they say, money talks. Between you and me, Il Duce is receiving far more than the museum is."

Beneath Brody's arm was a suitcase stuffed with lira.

"Oh, I forgot to tell you," Brody said. "Stefansson has asked me to extend a very cordial invitation to you to join the Explorers' Club. But then, it was the only thing he could do after your retrieval of the manuscript and your reinstatement at Princeton."

"Tell him," Indy said, "that I don't want to belong to any organization that would have me for a member."

They went directly to the second floor, where they were to meet the museum's acting director at the exhibit and make the exchange.

"I'm anxious to see the skull," Brody said happily as they neared the pedestal with its glass case. "I've seen photos, of course, but from what you describe, they simply don't do it justice."

"It gives me the spooks," Indy said. "I don't think I'll be visiting the exhibit for some ti—"

He stopped in midsentence, his hands in his pockets, his mouth open, staring at the display case. It was empty. A card placed inside had a single word in Italian.

Ruba.

"I'll bet it's being cleaned or something for the exchange," Brody said hopefully. "I'm sure that's it. Or they could be boxing it up, making it safe to ship."

Caramia's heels clicked briskly on the marble floor as she crossed the room toward them. Her dark hair was pinned in a bun, and on the lapel of her businesslike brown jacket was a miniature fasces, matching the ones on the double doors.

"Gentlemen," she said. "I'm sorry I could not reach

you before you arrived. I left word with Rinaldi at your hotel, but you had not yet checked in."

"Just tell me what this word means," Brody said.

"Don't you know, Marcus?" Indy asked. Then he smiled and said: "*Stolen.*"

AFTERWORD

Although *Indiana Jones and the Philosopher's Stone* is obviously a work of fiction, many of the things that Indy encounters in this adventure are based in fact. The descriptions of the Princeton University campus and the American Museum of Natural History in the 1930s, for example, are based on contemporary material such as the guides published by the Works Progress Administration. The following is for those interested in the subjects and the historical figures that Indy's adventure deals with.

Alchemy

Alchemy, the ancient pseudoscience that laid the foundation for modern chemistry, has all the elements of the classic quest: secret knowledge, arcane rituals, and the promise of unimaginable power and wealth. It is equally concerned with the material (the transmutation of base metals into gold through the fabled philosopher's stone) and the spiritual (a path by which adepts could hope to purify their souls).

Alchemical success stories are invariably apocryphal—such as the tale of Nicholas and Perenelle Flamel, who succeeded because their hearts were pure—but they have been enough to lure generations of practitioners into the study of obscure texts and to spend long hours in foul-smelling laboratories. And although alchemy may seem like a fool's quest to modern sensibilities, it has been taken seriously by a surprising number of practitioners.

Interest in alchemy was renewed early in this century, for example, when Lord Rutherford, the eminent English physician, succeeded in transmuting nitrogen into oxygen using high-energy radioactivity, which refuted the prevailing scientific opinion that transmutation was an impossibility.

The Nazis and the Italian Fascists both launched serious investigations into turning lead or other materials into gold, with the aim of funding their war machines.

Erich von Ludendorff, a fellow conspirator of Hitler's during the Munich uprising, organized "Company 164" to support the efforts of German alchemist Franz Tausand as a means of funding the Nazi Party. Tausand was arrested in 1929 for fraud. In 1931, following a sensational trial, Tausand was sentenced to four years in prison. While awaiting trial, however, Tausand allegedly made gold under close supervision at the Munich mint.

In 1936 Mussolini sent Fascist scientists to investigate a demonstration staged by Dunikovski, a Polish engineer who claimed that he had discovered a new kind of radiation—Z waves—that could turn sand into gold. Although the Italians declined to participate in Dunikovski's scheme (he had been convicted of fraud in 1931 for making similar claims), an Anglo-French syndicate was formed to bring sand from Africa to be treated in England. World War II intervened, however, and the plan was never put into practice. Also in the late 1930s, a London osteopath by the name of Archibald Cockren was reported to have made gold by using the Twelve Keys of Basil Valentine, a fifteenth-century German monk. Cockren, however, was killed during the blitz, and his secret apparently died with him.

Although the origins of alchemy are obscure, it seems to have emerged at roughly the same time in Egypt and China, about two thousand years ago. The concept of a "philosopher's stone" originated in China, where alchemy was associated with Taoism. Gold produced by a philosopher's stone was believed to have the power to cure disease and prolong life, and this idea was eventually picked up by Arab alchemists. Along the way other philosophies, such as the Aristotelian concept of four basic elements (earth, water, air, and fire), were grafted on, as well as the Arabic theory that all metals were composed of a balance of sulfur and mercury. Much of the spiritual side of alchemy came from the Gnostics, who envisioned a life-and-death struggle between good and evil in the chemical processes they described.

Alchemy became a curious mixture of religion, science, and cultural belief. By the second century Alexandria had become the international center for alchemy, where the supposed secrets of transmuting metals were carefully guarded by the temple priests. When the institutional study of alchemy came to an end in the fourth century with the destruction of the academy and great library at Alexandria, alchemists went underground. Alchemical texts became purposefully obscure, enigmatic, and couched in riddles that only the initiated could hope to decipher.

During the Middle Ages and the Renaissance, the invention of alchemy was usually attributed to Hermes Trismegistus. Some 36,000 alchemical texts (chief among which is the Emerald Tablet) were ascribed to Hermes, himself an enigmatic figure associated with the Egyptian god Thoth. Hermes, in fact, appears in so many different guises that it is impossible to list them all. This attribution of alchemy to an ancient lineage gave alchemy some badly needed credibility, something that all good quest stories require.

Although practitioners of the Great Work would recognize many of the devices used in a modern laboratory—flasks, retorts, and alembics were all devised by alchemists—those adepts of another time might recognize as well the symbols of their search as they have been incorporated into modern psychology. C. G. Jung, for example, was fascinated by the richness of alchemical symbolism: dragons, snakes, pelicans tearing at their own breasts, the incestuous marriage of brother and sister. It is in this wealth of myth and metaphor, perhaps, that the enduring contribution of alchemy to the human experience lies.

The Voynich Manuscript

Voynich may indeed be the world's most mysterious occult manuscript, having been studied unsuccessfully by generations of seers, scholars, and code breakers. It has even drawn the attention of the United States' most secret intelligence organization, the National Security Agency. Since 1968 the manuscript has been housed in the Beinecke Rare Book Room at Yale. Its value is estimated at between one-quarter and one-half million dollars.

The history of Voynich up to 1933 closely follows that related to Indy by the rare book dealer and others. Major John M. Manly, the noted Chaucerian scholar and army intelligence officer, is a historical figure who did much to debunk the pseudoscholarly research that had been published about the manuscript in the 1920s and 1930s. In 1921, for example, scholar William Newbold made headlines with his claim that the manuscript was the work of Roger Bacon and detailed the inventions of the microscope and telescope centuries before they were known to exist.

The angel-communing English occultists John Dee and Edward Kelley, who are believed to have sold the manuscript at Prague sometime before 1608, are also historical figures who often appear—in a curious mixture of charlatanism and belief—in occult histories. The Shew Stone is a real artifact, currently housed at the British Museum along with small amounts of gold that, as the stories have it, were made by English alchemists.

One of the joys of research is discovering new or unsuspected information, and this occurred early in the research for *Indiana Jones and the Philosopher's Stone.*

After reading Terrence McKenna's delightful account of Voynich in *The Archaic Revival,* I made a routine inter-library loan request based on a bibliographical note that listed a Department of Commerce publication on Voynich. After a lengthy search, the desired publication was finally delivered by my local university library. *The Voynich Manuscript: An Elegant Enigma,* by Mary D'Empirio, proved to be a 1978 report commissioned by the National Security Agency. D'Empirio's account is perhaps the best compilation about Voynich, but its only conclusion is that the manuscript deserves further study.

Although many have claimed decipherment over the years—and, more recently, sophisticated computer programs have been brought to bear on the task—the manuscript remains unreadable. Voynich seems to be either an elaborate historical joke containing nothing more than gibberish, or a real mystery containing the closely guarded secret of a past age.

The U.S.S. Macon

The 1930s was the age of the airship, and the U.S. Navy dirigible *Macon* represented the zenith of lighter-than-air technology. She was also the largest aircraft of any kind ever built—she weighed nearly a quarter of a million pounds—and, at 785 feet, was as long as three of today's Boeing 747s.

Her rigid aluminum frame was filled with helium—much safer than the explosive hydrogen that the German Zeppelin company was forced to use, since the United States controlled the world's helium supply—and in her belly she carried five small fighter planes. Her maiden flight occurred in 1933, just three weeks after her sister ship, the U.S.S. *Akron*, was lost in a thunderstorm over the North Atlantic with all but three of her seventy-six-man crew. The wreck was blamed on a violent air pocket and a faulty altimeter that still read several hundred feet when the *Akron* hit the water.

Designed by a team of German engineers and built by the Goodyear-Zeppelin Corporation, both the *Akron* and the *Macon* were designed as aerial platforms for scout aircraft. The tiny Sparrowhawk fighters could search an ocean lane one hundred miles wide, at seventy-five miles per hour.

The design of the *Macon* represented several improvements over her ill-fated sister ship: more speed, slightly better lift, and the use of a new gelatin-latex fabric for her twelve gas cells instead of goldbeater's skin, a material fashioned from animal intestine.

Although the *Macon* was never used in wartime, she proved her search capability when her commander, Herbert V. Wiley, undertook an unauthorized mission to find vacationing President Franklin D. Roosevelt in the Pacific Ocean, en route to Hawaii. They found FDR on the cruiser *Houston* approximately 1,500 miles from shore, and the Sparrowhawk pilots, knowing the president enjoyed regular newspapers, dropped the latest San Francisco papers on the deck of the cruiser. Roosevelt was impressed, but the navy was not amused; it is said that only the president's intercession prevented Wiley from being court-martialed.

On February 12, 1935, the *Macon* was returning to Moffett Field near San Francisco when a violent gust of wind collapsed her upper tail fin and the edges of the fin punctured three helium cells. She settled into the Pacific about five miles off Point Sur. A radioman and a mess steward died in the wreck, but the other eighty-three crew members aboard were rescued by naval vessels conducting fleet exercises nearby.

The watery grave of the *Macon,* once the pride of the U.S. Navy, remained undisturbed for more than half a century.

In 1980 a commercial fisherman winched up a two-foot piece of yellow aluminum girder off of Point Sur. The girder was eventually displayed as a mysterious curiosity on the wall of a restaurant near Monterey where Marie Wiley Ross—daughter of the *Macon*'s commander—eventually spotted it and recognized the piece of twisted aluminum for what it was. This set off a chain of events that culminated on June 24, 1990, when the navy sent its deep submersible *Sea Cliff* to the site. What was left of the *Macon* was located within fifteen minutes, including the skeletal remains of three Sparrowhawk fighters, at a depth of 1,450 feet.

Italo Balbo

Italo Balbo, an Italian Fascist leader and aviator, was born on June 6, 1896. His most memorable accomplishment was not the organized mass demonstration flights across the Atlantic to Brazil and the United States in 1930 and 1933, but the affection with which many Americans still regard him.

Although it took Balbo's armada nearly two weeks to make it from Italy to Chicago during the second transatlantic flight because of weather delays and other considerations, their elapsed flying time was an electrifying forty-eight hours. Balbo was hailed as a hero, and more comparisons were made to Columbus than to Mussolini; in Chicago a major thoroughfare and a monument to the crossing still bear his name. In 1935 he was awarded the Distinguished Flying Cross, a singular honor for one who was not an American citizen. His admirers included Dwight Eisenhower, a young military officer in 1933 assigned to host the Balbo armada.

The SM.55 twin-hulled flying boats that Balbo's squadrons used established a series of endurance and distance records. The flying boats that were produced by Savoia-Marchetti in the 1920s and 1930s proved to be so reliable that many were put into service by some of the first commercial airlines, and some military models were still in use through the dark days of World War II.

Mussolini appointed Balbo governor of Libya in 1933, out of a sense of jealousy, perhaps, for his lieutenant's popularity in Italy and America. The appointment crushed Balbo, who was firm in his conviction that his place was as a pioneering aviator and not the administrator of an Italian colony. Balbo died in Libya on June 28, 1940, when his plane was mistakenly shot down by anti-aircraft fire from his own troops.

Mussolini's end was to come five years later, during the closing months of World War II. After his military disasters in Greece and North Africa, the Fascist Party had him arrested in 1943, but the Germans rescued him and set him up as the head of a puppet government in northern Italy. On April 28, 1945, after being captured by Italian partisans while attempting to flee the Allied advance, Mussolini and his mistress, Clara Petacci, were

shot by a firing squad. Their bodies were hung in a public square in Milan.

On Columbus Day, 1973, the fortieth anniversary
of Balbo's transatlantic crossing, fifty-eight surviving
members of the *atlantici* accompanied Mayor Richard
Daley in a parade down the streets of Chicago.

About the Author

MAX MCCOY is an award-winning journalist and author whose Bantam novels include *The Sixth Rider* and *Sons of Fire*. He lives in Pittsburg, Kansas, where he is currently at work on the next Indiana Jones novel.

⊰ INDIANA JONES ⊱

Bold adventurer, swashbuckling explorer,
Indy unravels the mysteries of the past at a time when
dreams could still come true. Now, in a series officially
licensed from Lucasfilm, we will learn what shaped
Indiana Jones into the hero he is today!

THE PERIL AT DELPHI by Rob MacGregor
_____ 28931-4 $4.99/$5.99 in Canada

THE DANCE OF THE GIANTS by Rob MacGregor
_____ 29035-5 $4.99/$5.99 in Canada

THE SEVEN VEILS by Rob MacGregor
_____ 29334-6 $4.99/$5.99 in Canada

THE GENESIS DELUGE by Rob MacGregor
_____ 29502-0 $4.99/$5.99 in Canada

THE UNICORN'S LEGACY by Rob MacGregor
_____ 29666-3 $4.99/$5.99 in Canada

THE INTERIOR WORLD by Rob MacGregor
_____ 29966-2 $4.99/$5.99 in Canada

THE SKY PIRATES by Martin Caidin
_____ 56192-8 $4.99/$5.99 in Canada

THE WHITE WITCH by Martin Caidin
_____ 56194-4 $4.99/$5.99 in Canada

- -

Ask for these books at your local bookstore or use this page to order.

Please send me the books I have checked above. I am enclosing $_____ (add $2.50 to
cover postage and handling). Send check or money order, no cash or C.O.D.'s, please.

Name _____

Address _____

City/State/Zip _____

Send order to: Bantam Books, Dept. FL 7, 2451 S. Wolf Rd., Des Plaines, IL 60018
Allow four to six weeks for delivery.
Prices and availability subject to change without notice.   FL 7 5/95

THE SAGA OF THE FIRST AMERICANS

*The spellbinding epic of adventure
at the dawn of history*

by William Sarabande

THE EDGE OF THE WORLD

____56028-X $5.99/$6.99 in Canada

____26889-9 BEYOND THE SEA OF ICE $5.99/$6.99 in Canada

____27159-8 CORRIDOR OF STORMS $5.99/$6.99 in Canada

____28206-9 FORBIDDEN LAND $5.99/$6.99 in Canada

____28579-3 WALKERS OF THE WIND $5.99/$6.99 in Canada

____29105-X THE SACRED STONES $5.99/$6.99 in Canada

____29106-8 THUNDER IN THE SKY $5.99/$6.99 in Canada

Also by William Sarabande

____25802-8 WOLVES OF THE DAWN $5.99/$7.50 in Canada

Ask for these books at your local bookstore or use this page to order.

Please send me the books I have checked above. I am enclosing $____(add $2.50 to cover postage and handling). Send check or money order, no cash or C.O.D.'s, please.

Name _____

Address _____

City/State/Zip _____

Send order to: Bantam Books, Dept. DO 1, 2451 S. Wolf Rd., Des Plaines, IL 60018
Allow four to six weeks for delivery.
Prices and availability subject to change without notice.   DO 1 5/95